Helen Roberta Saneabi
(8-20-01)

Tales of the Wailing Winds

Tales of the Wailing Winds

A Collection of Short Stories

Helen Roberta Sanecki

VANTAGE PRESS
New York

These stories are works of fiction. Any similarities between the characters appearing in them and any real person, living or dead, is purely coincidental.

Cover design by Susan Thomas

Published by Vantage Press, Inc.
516 West 34th Street, New York, New York 10001

Manufactured in the United States of America
ISBN: 0-533-13668-7

Library of Congress Catalog Card No.: 00-91600

0 9 8 7 6 5 4 3 2 1

In memory of my family

Contents

Preface   ix

The Old Jennings Place   1
The Stallion   4
The Man in the Low Seat   11
Lilia   13
King of the Hill   38
But for the Grace of God   47
A Gift of Friendship   57
Good-Bye, Ellie Kaye   67
Beyond the Summers, into the Sunset   100
Vengeance Is Not Sweet   111
A Tale of Puppy Love   118
Oh, Joey, Can You Hear Me Cry?   132
There Comes a Day of Reckoning   155
The Allotment   166
Sammy   186

Preface

The direction from which the wind blows, East or West, South or North, determines the pattern and degree of force it will take. This can range from complete calm to slight breezes, through various speeds of gales, up to severe storms. The consequences can be beneficial, like a gentle rain during the growing season or devastating as a tornado causing widespread destruction and death. So runs the course of all lives. The direction and pattern taken determine the consequence. It can be a long, serene, fulfilling life or one of high pressures, ups and downs, tortured mind, ending in violence and death.

Tales of the Wailing Winds

The Old Jennings Place

The fences are down, their posts rotted away by the elements and time. Laid low by howling winds and banks of drifting snow, the falling posts took the fence lines down with them. Between the squares of broken, rusting wires grow tall grasses and weeds, alongside thorny blackberry bushes and wild apple trees. Once these fences guarded fields of golden grain—wheat, oats, rye, and barley, gently waving in the northern breeze—fields of corn, clover, and alfalfa, orchards, and gardens. No longer checked and repaired every spring, the fences lie where they fall.

The fields seed themselves—each season brings its own potpourri of growing plants. Spring bursts forth in various shades of green, then sprinkles the fields with bright yellow dandelions. Summer overflows with lacy white wild carrot intermingled with black-eyed Susans and white daises. Wild strawberry vines creep along the sunny hillsides. Goldenrod dominates the late summer and burdock and thistle grow purple blooms, the size of which you have never seen. When the milkweed pods began to burst and shed their silky, downy seeds, summer is coming to an end. A short while and the whole landscape is arrayed in brilliant shades of yellow, orange, and red; then all is stripped by the winds and the seeds scattered over the fields. Spring brings all to life again.

The winding, rippling stream is gone—the springs ran dry, leaving a stony path among the evergreens. Huge stone boulders lie in dried mud holes. No longer do brookies or rainbow swim under the wooden bridge. No ducks nest in marshes along the stream or swim in its waters with their broods of fuzzy yellow ducklings. No cattle line up at the banks for a drink of clear, cool water. Ferns cover the cow paths, some with fronds shoulder-high. The stately elms, which grew throughout the pasture, have all fallen prey to Dutch elm disease. Their gray trunks hover over the land like giant ghosts. Woodpeckers chip away at the rotting wood, some searching for insects; others, cutting out holes large enough to nest their young.

The barns stand empty, the roofs leaking, the windows broken. Under the eaves, swallows tend their young, undisturbed. The odor of molding hay permeates the whole area. In the cattle barn, the stalls are falling apart. An old straw hat lies in one of the mangers; another holds two milking stools. The cream separator stands in the milk room, just as it was left when the last pail of milk was run through for cream. A large white enamel pan, where cats lined up for warm milk every morning and evening, lies upside down near the separator. In the horse barn, a set of harnesses still hangs on the wall and a pitchfork stands in the corner near the big wooden door. Elderberry bushes hide the door to the henhouse, and animal burrows, from mice to woodchuck, can be seen everywhere.

The house stands on its hilly pedestal; its cedar siding, once the white of freshly fallen snow, has turned a weather-beaten dingy gray. The windows, their shades torn, are covered with dust and grime no rains can wash away. A swallow has built her nest over the front door, and spiders spin silvery threads across the threshold. Hollyhocks crowd around the picket fence; wild grasses overrun the walkways. Near the entrance gate stands a huge gray stone with faint traces of once big black letters spelling out: **ROBERT JENNINGS.**

The old homestead stands forlorn and haunting, yet when evening comes and the sun is moving towards the hills the windows of the old house capture and reflect the golden rays of the setting sun, returning to the old gray house some of its inviting warmth of former days—a certain glow, like the promise of another tomorrow, another generation.

The Stallion

On a hot August night, with my bedroom window wide open, thundering hoofbeats of a galloping horse awakened me from a deep sleep. I glanced at the clock on the bedside table. The time was 1:30. What was a horse doing out on the road, galloping, in the middle of the night?

I jumped out of bed and ran to the window. Abruptly the galloping ceased. A large lamp on the television antenna lit up the yard around the house and the driveway and provided me with a clear view of the whole area. I did not see a horse anywhere. I returned to bed and pondered, *Where did the horse come from? And did it have a rider?*

On the three-mile stretch of gravel road that ran between two main highways lay four large tracts of farmland. None of the farms had horses anymore. All the farmers used tractors in their farming operations. A private club, on the main highway to the west, had a riding stable and several horses. Their section of property was enclosed with a high wire fence and the main entrance guarded with two large iron gates, which could only be opened with a membership pass. It was unlikely that one of their horses would be out on the road this time of night.

As I lay in bed, wide awake, tossing and turning, my thoughts drifted back to the autumn of 1931. It was a time of the Great Depression, and Father had lost his job at the Lincoln automotive plant in Detroit, where he had worked for many years. Up to this time, a neighbor had been working our land on shares; now Father was taking over the farming operations. But before Father could farm he had to have a team of horses.

When Father returned home after the layoff, he brought with him $200. It was his last pay and a small sum he had accumulated in the shop's employees' savings fund. It was the only money he had. With this money he bought two horses from Jake Simpson, a horse breeder and trader whose farm was just a short distance down the road from our place.

When Jake delivered the horses that afternoon, Father was not home. He had gone to town to buy some tools. The horses were two beautiful Belgian stallions with short shiny chestnut hair and creamy white manes and tails. Both held their heads high and appeared very alert, turning their heads in all directions as if surveying their new surroundings.

Mother escorted Jake and the horses to our pasture, and I tagged along. The pasture stretched out over a large area and enclosed the large sprawling unpainted barn and several small buildings, Jake untied the animals, and the spirited horses took off at a high speed, galloping around and around the pasture, their white tails flung high and their manes flowing in the wind. I was fascinated with the beautiful creatures. "Do they have names?" I asked Jake.

"Yes, they have. Nip and Jim. Jim has the wider blaze," Jake told me, pointing to the white patch running down the horse's face from his mane to the tip of his nose.

Jake left and Mother and I returned to the house. As we stepped on the back porch, thunder rumbled in the distance and a gold streak of lightning zigzagged down to earth from the black sky on the horizon.

Realizing her mistake, Mother reproached herself, "I should have asked Jake to take the horses to the stable and put them in their stalls. They cannot be left out in the storm. Electrical charges in the ground can flow up into a horse's body through his hooves, making him a lightning rod, and kill him."

I went to the granary with Mother. She filled a wooden bucket with oats and handed it to me, saying, "See if you can coax those horses into the stable."

As I entered the pasture, the storm had reached our farm in all its fury. The whole sky appeared to be hissing and rumbling. The horses, frightened, whinnied and pranced at the gate through which they had entered the pasture. I was more frightened than the horses—I was scared half to death.

I was a defiant twelve-year-old, and Mother was constantly threatening me with, "Young lady, one of these days God is going to punish you for all that sassing and disobeying your mother." As torrential rains drenched me, Mother's words came back to haunt me. Would this be my day of doom? Suddenly a sharp, violent, detonating crack sent me to the ground. I was sure that God had struck me with one of his thunderbolts. Then, as quickly as it came, the storm stopped. Only the rushing waters of the stream below the barn could be heard. I raised my head and saw the large oak tree on the hill with its trunk ripped right down the middle. I raised myself off the ground and picked up the bucket with the remaining oats. Half of the grain was spilled on the ground, and the horses were lapping it up. The horses realized there were more oats in the bucket and followed me to the stable.

It was the most terrifying experience of my whole life, but it did not make me a more obedient child, only a more determined one. I made up my mind that if, ever again,

Mother asked me to go out in a storm, I would tell her, "Why don't you go out there yourself!"

Mother had made a mistake, but Father committed an even greater error. He took a great risk when he bought the three-year-old stallions. Nip and Jim would have to be castrated before they could be broken in as a team of draft horses. There was the chance of losing them . . . and we almost did.

We did not have a licensed veterinarian in our area. The farmer who came with Jake to do the deed had only the veterinary knowledge that had been passed down to him through his father and grandfather. The surgical procedure turned out to be traumatic for both Nip and Jim.

For many hours Father and the two men hovered over the suffering horses in the barn; in the house, Mother and I were down on our knees, praying that the horses would not die. If our horses did not survive, there was no money to buy another team. The total sum of money in our home that day was a five-dollar bill Father had received for a crate of eggs and a can of cream he had sold at the country store. How could Father work the land if he did not have horses? Mother was terribly upset and very angry with Father for not insisting that Jake have the stallions neutered before he paid him the $200.

Nip and Jim survived the ordeal and became a work team Father was proud to own. With fondest memories of many sleigh rides down snowy country roads with the two beautiful Belgian horses I finally fell asleep.

Shortly after eight o'clock the next morning, I heard a dog barking in the backyard and got up to investigate. The neighbor's black mongrel was running around my garden, yapping ferociously at a horse. The horse, a chestnut stallion, stood in the middle of the garden, chomping on crunchy carrots and ignoring the excited mutt running around him in a frenzy. The chestnut coloring of his coat, white blaze on his head, and white stockings on his legs all reminded me of our Belgians. He could have been one of them, except he was somewhat smaller.

"Blackie, you go home!" I shouted at the dog.

He made no attempt to leave and continued circling the garden, barking viciously. Again I shouted at him, "You go home, you bad doggy!" and threw a large twig at him. Blackie turned his long bushy tail between his legs and slowly retreated home.

Unafraid and holding his head high, the stallion walked up to me with pompous dignity. He followed me to the back porch, where the previous afternoon I had set out two pails, under the eaves, to catch rainwater for houseplants. The rain had filled them both to the brim. This morning, they were empty. Sometime during the night, the horse had drunk up all the water, and now he had his head down in one of the pails, looking for more. I filled the water trough at the outside pump for him and returned to the house to call the sheriff.

No one had reported a missing horse to the sheriff's office. Deputy Brown took my name, address, and telephone number in case they received a call later that morning. Within the hour, I heard a vehicle drive into the yard.

A tan pickup truck, pulling a matching horse carrier, parked in the driveway, and a couple alit from the truck's cab. Both wore identical fancy brown-and-tan riding outfits with wide-brimmed felt hats and high brown leather boots. The man immediately went to the back of the trailer and pulled out a wide ramp. I walked up to the woman, a tall, slender, elegant blonde. She greeted me with an introduction: "We're Cordelia and Randolph Van Hogan, the new owners of the Arnold ranch."

The old Arnold place was a 320-acre spread with a colorful fieldstone house, two large red barns, and several smaller buildings. It was considered the most beautiful setting in the township. The west end of the property bordered on a main highway, and the north end, with all the buildings, faced the gravel road that ran by my house. The stallion had strayed two miles from home.

"How did your horse get out?" I asked Cordelia.

"He pushed open the corral gate. It must not have been closed properly. Randolph found him missing when he went to bring him into the stable this morning. A veterinarian is coming to emasculate him."

Emasculate? I had not heard the term before. Still remembering what had happened to our Belgian stallions, whether it was emasculation, castration, or neutering, to me it meant the mutilation of a horse—depriving him of his masculine vigor and spirit.

Cordelia and I watched the stallion, his proud head bowed, his stride hesitant, climb the ramp into the trailer. I turned to her and said, "What a magnificent Belgian!"

"Oh, no!" she cried out in an arrogant voice that told me I had just greatly insulted her horse. "Prince Jay is not a Belgian. He's a purebred Arabian, a noble horse." She paused for a moment, then added, "And he's going to be my very own personal riding horse."

I wanted to shout, "Hoity-toity!" but the woman was right. Prince Jay belonged to the nobility of the horse kingdom. His ancestors were the oldest domesticated species in the world, dating back to Old Testament times and the land of Arabia, where they ran wild. Arabian sheiks caught the young foals and tamed them. They considered the horses a gift from God.

The Arabian horses served their masters well, and warriors of all eras rode them in battle. The sheiks used them in fierce tribal wars, fought under the blistering desert sun. The prophet Muhammad chose Arabian mares for his campaigns. An Arabian charger carried George Washington through the American Revolution, and an Arabian desert stallion accompanied Napoléon on his long retreat from Moscow.

Truly the Arabian horse came from an aristocracy of lofty lineage and so did Prince Jay; but before the morning came to an end, the magnificent high-spirited stallion would be transformed to a gelding. He would become docile, calm, and obedient to the commands of a woman who wanted a noble animal for her very own riding horse, but first she had to make sure she could control him.

Bibliography

Album of Horses. Henry, Marguerite. Rand McNally & Company, 1978.
Horses: 24 Posters. Great Britain: Colour Library Books Ltd., 1983.

The Man in the Low Seat

In the early 1940s, I worked in a tuberculosis sanitorium owned by the city of Detroit. Tuberculosis, one of the greatest killers ever known to man, was one of the leading causes of death in the metropolitan area. The hospital facilities had a capacity of 844 beds and the services of 478 employees, an all-white work force. Not until civil service examinations became policy for the selection of employees did a black man report to work at the sanatorium.

I was the dietary office clerk on duty at the cash register when the cafeteria opened for breakfast that Monday. A steady line of nurses, aides, and orderlies came through the door, all in crisp white uniforms. They were the morning shift, scheduled for the wards at seven o'clock. The group was unusually noisy. Angry voices protested the arrival of the new orderly on Ward II: "You all know we're getting a nigger this morning?" "That's what civil service done." "They gave him a room in the men's quarters." "Probably brought bedbugs with him and Lord knows what else."

These were some of the sputterings from resentful orderlies who would be sharing living quarters and working with the black man. I rang up each tray as it came down the line: orange juice, bananas, cereal, scrambled eggs, crisp bacon, browned sausages, country fried potatoes, hot cinnamon buns, toast and jelly, milk, coffee, and tea. The stainless-steel pans on the long food counter held many choices.

The initial line went through quickly with only a few stragglers still coming in when a black man walked into the

11

cafeteria, a slender man about five-foot-five wearing a shabby brown suit. The coat had a button missing; the pants were frayed at the cuffs, the brown plaid shirt badly faded. His jet-black hair was curled tightly to the scalp, his dark-skinned face clean-shaven and shiny, his thick lips slightly everted.

He selected a cinnamon roll and asked for a cup of coffee. Then he reached into his coat pocket and pulled out a piece of white paper. The note had the gold monogram of the superintendent of nurses. A short message read: "Willie Dawson is a new orderly on Ward II. He has been cleared for credit until the first payday." I clipped the register receipt to the note and slipped it under my money box.

Willie Dawson picked up his tray and stood for a moment looking around the dining room with the round tables, each seating up to eight persons. He spotted a small square table with a single chair at the far end of the room and he headed in that direction. The chair at the square table was shorter than any other chair in the dining room. Also, the table stood under a large window overlooking the entrance leading from the main road to the hospital morgue. Here undertakers came in the morning to pick up the stiffs, as the orderlies called the patients they brought down from the infirmary who had not made it through the night. No one ever sat at that table.

While an atmosphere of hostility and arrogance surrounded many a table in the dining room, a halo of humility hung over the low chair where the black man sat down, clasped his palms together, bowed his head, and gave thanks to the Lord for his cinnamon roll and coffee.

Lilia

On a sunny morning in the summer of 1914, a five-year-old Polish girl stood by a well in front of her grandparents' cottage, watching her mother draw a bucket of cool spring water. The girl's name was Lilia. Lilia had her mother's brown eyes and raven-colored hair, which hung down her shoulders in long pigtails. The bows of white satin ribbon tightly fastened at the end of each plait were a gift from her father, sent from America. The identical soft blue paisley skirts and white voile blouses she and her mother wore that day had come in the same package with the ribbon.

Three years had gone by since Adam Kramek left Lilia and her mother with his parents and sailed for America. His departing words to his family were, "As soon as I have enough money to buy us a place of our own, I'll be back. It shouldn't be more than three years."

Lilia was only two years old at the time of her father's departure and did not remember him, but that did not keep her from anxiously waiting for the day of his return, eyeing every stranger she encountered, hoping he was her daddy coming back to her.

In recent days, several strange men had passed through the village, scouting the area, asking questions, and recording information in little black books. The villagers suspiciously referred to them as spies. Although the day was sunny, ominous clouds hung over the land, threatening the village and its people. Information had come through that a Serb had assassinated the archduke of Austria. The village was rife with rumors of an impending Russian mobilization and war.

As Lilia follower her mother toward the cottage door, she heard dogs barking in the distance and turned around to check what the commotion was all about. She saw two men coming down the main road, which ran through the center of the village, dividing it into two sections. One man took the road to the west; the other came east, a stocky man wearing a dark brown suit with a matching cap. He carried a brown leather case under his right arm.

"Look, Mama!" Lilia cried out. "There's a man coming down our road. It may be Daddy."

Maryanka Kramek looked at the short, swarthy man and answered, "No, my dear one, he's not your daddy. Your daddy is a tall, slender man, blond, and very handsome. That man is just another spy."

The two men entered every cottage along their route. They were emissaries from the provincial government in Lublin. Each carried with him a list of men in his section of the village and a special directive for the men from the officials at the Administrative Division of the province. The directive stated: "Every able-bodied man is to take an extra shirt with him and report to the county seat immediately. Only the old and the very young shall be exempt." The Polish village was a part of the Russian czar's territory, and Russia was mobilizing for war. Soon the screams and wailing of women were heard from all four corners of the once-peaceful village. Rumor became reality. Their men were off to war again.

When the man in the brown suit entered the Kramek cottage, he already knew there were three men in the household—Thomas Kramek, Lilia's grandfather, and her two uncles Victor and Stephen.

Thomas Kramek greeted the visitor with the customary "Good day, sir."

The government agent did not respond to the greeting but immediately confronted the grandfather with, "There are two young men in this household, ages eighteen and twenty. Is that correct?"

"Yes, that is correct," the grandfather answered.

The agent looked around the small dark room and asked, "Where are they now?"

"They are out in the barn, putting up hay in the loft."

"Call them in," the agent demanded.

Victor and Stephen returned to the cottage with great apprehension. They stood before the agent in a state of shock, stunned by the realization that they were being conscripted for military duty and terrified as to what awaited them in the days to come. Their homespun linen shirts, soaked with sweat from the intense heat in the haymow, clung to their hot bodies; perspiration dripped from their suntanned faces and mingled with bitter tears that were difficult to hold back.

The agent wasted no time. In a cold, authoritative manner and tone of voice, he addressed the Kramek brothers: "Each of you is to take the extra shirt with you and report to the Provincial Headquarters in Lublin at once!" Then, turning to their father, he stated, "An army of Austrian soldiers from the Galician region is heading this way. We expect fighting in this area. Find the safest place for your family to be when that time comes. You probably should dig a trench." Then, turning on his heel, the man want out the door and continued down the road to the next cottage, leaving behind a family in emotional chaos.

Lilia stayed close to her mother, snuggling up against her side and holding tightly onto her hand, as she watched her grandmother sobbing uncontrollably and her aunts,

Frances and Anna, trying to console the grandmother while quietly weeping tears of their own.

Weary and overwhelmed by the events of the morning, Maryanka walked her daughter to a bench, standing under one of the windows in the room, and they both sat down. Lilia climbed up on her mother's lap, flung her arms around her neck, and laid her head on her mother's shoulder. From the time Lilia first spotted the man in the brown suit coming down the road toward their cottage she had witnessed all that happened that morning and heard every word exchanged between the adults—Lilia was terrified!

Thomas Kramek went to the barn to feed the horses and get the wagon ready for the trip to Lublin.

Victor and Stephen headed for the Vistula River, which ran only a short distance from their home, to bathe in its cool, fast-flowing waters. After a quick dip, they returned to the cottage, put on clean sets of clothes, and sat down at the large round oak table with the rest of the family.

As the family ate their lunch of potato dumplings with fried salt pork cracklings, prune-filled cake, and tea, an eerie silence replaced the usual lively conversations the family carried on during their meals. This day, each family member was engrossed in his or her own private thoughts. All were well versed in the tragic events of Poland's history and the suffering endured by its people during previous wars. History books and personal stories passed down from generation to generation told it all. There were tales of men who left for war and never returned, of families who searched for sons all their lives, never found them, never learned where they were buried.

There were tales of hardship and of horrors inflicted on those who remained in the village—their buildings were burned, their livestock slaughtered, even horses and dogs killed for meat by hungry soldiers. Some villagers survived, only to be stricken by famine and dying of starvation; others perished in epidemics of cholera and typhus. But, somehow, the Kramek family name survived and was passed on to the next generation.

Time and again Poland was invaded—by Mongolians and Turks; by Swedes, Lithuanians, and Ruthenians. There were devastating raids by the fierce Tatars from the East, who plundered the land and laid it to waste. There were raids by the Russians, whose fighters on horseback, the dreaded Cossacks, drove panic-stricken peasants before them with whips and sabers.

Finally, in 1795, Poland was partitioned for the third time by Austria, Prussia, and Russia and disappeared as an independent state from the maps of Europe.

The country died a bloody, tragic death, but the spirit of nationalism lived on in its people. They preserved their Polish language for more than a hundred years. They kept all their customs and traditions and devoutly practiced their Catholic faith, nor did they lose hope as they waited for the day when their country would be returned to them and they would be a free people again. Such was the heritage and the legacy of the five-year-old Lilia Kramek in the summer of 1914.

The meal ended with a prayer, led by Lilia's grandfather. The whole family joined in asking God's mercy in sparing the village and its people from the terrible consequences of war. They prayed for a quick and lasting peace, and they prayed that God would watch over Victor and Stephen that they might return safely home, whole in body and sound of mind and spirit.

For a few precious moments the family huddled together with their arms around one another, but the goodbyes were cut short. The first contingent of village men was already on its way to Lublin. Victor and Stephen had to leave.

They picked up their extra shirts and headed for the wagon their father had been waiting for them by the side of the road. Neither stopped to look back.

As the newly conscripted army of men moved along the main road toward the county seat, their families lined up along the way and watched until the last man and wagon disappeared into the horizon. The four Kramek women and Lilia returned home and, in silence, awaited the return of the grandfather.

Lilia was the first to speak, asking one question after another: "Mama, why did Granddaddy say that I could be a problem? Why must I stay in the house? Why can't anyone talk to me?"

"Your granddaddy will take up the matter with you when he returns, but, for now, be a good girl and do as he said. If anyone should come in and ask you any questions, just shake your head that you know nothing." The grandfather was a stern man, and Lilia was afraid to displease him. Her mother was sure she would obey the instruction.

Lilia was a quiet, well-behaved little girl. Living with a family of seven adults, she was considered to possess insight and understanding far advanced for her five years by all who knew her. And no one was more aware of this fact than her grandfather. He had observed her on many an occasion sizing up visitors to their home—sometimes immediately warming up to them in friendship; other times, remaining cool and distant. He noticed how keenly she listened in on adult conversations and seemed to comprehend what the discussions were all about. He watched her interactions with other children and noticed how frequently she instigated their activities and was their leader. There was no doubt in the grandfather's mind that Lilia was a precocious chid. This awareness caused Thomas Kramek much anxiety and made him uneasy and fearful, for the picturesque land surrounding the quiet village held many secrets and one was known to the Kramek family—the centuries-old secret of the caves, passed down through the generations who were born and lived on the ancestral lands. An unsettling question haunted the grandfather: did Lilia know about the caves, and if so, what did she know?

There was a time that when the name "Kramek" was called out responses echoed from all four corners of the village. Devastating raids by Tatars and Cossacks had reduced their numbers. Those who survived, survived because of the caves hidden in the escarpments of the Vistula River on the north side of the cottage. The limestone slopes, cut with deep ravines and caves and covered by white loess, provided a God-sent haven for the family during dangerous times.

All the way home from Lublin, Thomas Kramek pondered over his dilemma—to question Lilia or take the chance that she had no knowledge of the secret hideout. He decided not to question her. He felt that since she was a very curious child, she might look for the cave on her own and arouse suspicion. If the secret leaked out, the consequences could be catastrophic, leading to decimation, or even annihilation, of the family. From this day on, she would have to be watched closely and one of them would have to be with her at all times.

When Thomas arrived home, dusk was already settling on the land. The whole landscape looked deserted. Animals that normally would still be in the pastures or around the buildings were all locked up in the barns. As the horses pulled up to the barn, the wide doors swung open and Agnes Kramek came running out to meet her husband. His brother, Joseph, was with her. Greatly relieved that Thomas was safe, Agnes cried out, "Thank God you're back! We were expecting you hours ago and were terribly worried that something had happened to you."

"I stayed with the boys as long as I was permitted, then got caught in the congestion on the roads coming back home."

"Did you hear anything as to how far the situation has progressed?" Joseph asked.

"Some, but it's hard to tell, at this time, what is true and what is just a rumor. If all I heard is true, the situation is frightening."

"Why so?"

"The Russians do not have the necessary noncommissioned officers to help with the training of the new recruits."

"With the lack of schooling and all the illiteracy in Russia I am not surprised," Joseph responded.

"And that is not their only problem," Thomas continued. "There is also a shortage of artillery and ammunition. It is heartbreaking to see all those men being processed into an army, destined to meet its enemy most any time now and not have the military training and arms to protect themselves. They're innocents headed for the slaughter."

"We've been watching Russian soldiers massing on the border, across the river, since late afternoon," Joseph said. "It appears that they may be planning to encamp there for the night."

"I saw them, too, all along the river. They will be crossing in the morning, and they will be crossing the Vistula, right onto our road. It's a good thing we checked out and cleaned the cave last week. Did you get some supplies down there?"

"Yes, we did. The shelter is all set; when the time comes we have to use it."

At the break of dawn the following morning, while a gray mist slowly lifted from the valley, sounds of prancing horses woke up the Kramek family. Lilia was the first to jump out of bed and run into the kitchen, where two windows offered an excellent view of the village road. The approaching wave of horses, uniformed men, and horse-drawn carts with high wheels and carrying big black guns was an awesome sight. Lilia was both frightened and fascinated.

Soldiers, mounted on gray horses, led the procession. They wore uniforms of tan jackets and drab green pants, flat crown caps with visors, and knee-high black leather boots. Sabers in long brown leather cases hung at their right sides, with only their gold hilts exposed. These soldiers were a unit of the Russian cavalry.

The artillery section followed the cavalry; then came the foot soldiers in uniforms of solid green and with caps fastened under the chin with a leather strap. Each had a strapped tent cloth draped across his body down to the left hip, from which hung a brown leather pouch. Every man carried a rifle, which rested on his left shoulder and had a gray steel bayonet attached to the muzzle, pointing toward the sky. The eyes of a whole village were watching the military units that morning, but not one head turned to the right or the left. All stared straight ahead as they marched in a steady procession toward their destination.

Maryanka came up behind Lilia and put both arms around her daughter. She pulled her close to her bosom and held her tightly.

"I'm looking for Uncle Stephen," Lilia told her mother in an excited voice.

"You won't find Uncle Stephen in this group," her mother replied. "These soldiers are from the czar's regular army. They most likely came from Moscow. Uncle Stephen is with the new recruits in Lublin."

Stephen was Lilia's godfather and her favorite uncle. He bounced her on his knees and read children's stories and sang folk songs to her. He could keep her spellbound for many an hour with his colorful paper cut-outs of bird and flower designs. Whenever he visited the market town of Kazmierz Dolny, where he was well known for his artistic wicker-ware designs—from baskets to wall hangings—he brought a gift for her. She received boxes of delicious candy, which she shared with her playmates; a velvet burgundy vest, all embroidered with bright-colored yarns, which she wore to church on Sundays; and a doll with long braids dressed in the native costume of the province of Lubin. Lilia adored her Uncle Stephen.

Although the army that crossed the Vistula that morning did not stop in the village, the people knew that it was only a matter of time before soldiers would encamp along the river and on their land. During the days that followed, artillery bombardment from a distance could be heard in the village night and day, but the village, locked in by the steep limestone hills and the Vistula River, remained peaceful. It was an uneasy peace, and it was shattered one afternoon when a platoon of Russian soldiers decided to encamp for the night along the river and in the open fields of the village.

From the day the first soldiers passed through the village, Maryanka kept Lilia close at her side at all times. This afternoon, Maryanka became distracted by the arriving soldiers. It was only for a few minutes, but it was long enough for Lilia to slip away from her mother and leave the cottage. The distraught mother ran out into the field back of the cottage, frantically shouting, "Lilia! Lilia!"

A group of soldiers, milling around a campfire, heard Maryanka calling and waved to her to come forward. Hesitantly she headed toward the camp, and there was Lilia, sitting on a soldier's lap. Both were drinking tea from the same cup and taking turns at biting into the same hunk of black

Russian bread. Apprehensive and at a loss for words, Mary-anka stood still.

The soldier holding Lilia spoke first, "Don't be afraid, lady. I am not going to hurt your daughter. I have two little girls of my own, who are alone with their mother in a village not much larger than this."

Then another soldier spoke up: "You don't have to worry about this group. Many of us left small children behind when we were forced into military service. We're not interested in killing people and conquering lands. We just want to get it all over with and return home to our families."

As Lilia climbed down from the soldier's lap, he turned to her mother and laughed, "Your little girl thought I was her Uncle Stephen. I told her I couldn't be her Uncle Stephen, but I would be her Uncle Ivan as long as I stay in this area."

Thomas Kramek was returning home from a consultation with his brother, Joseph, when he spotted Maryanka and Lilia leaving the soldiers' camp. He was furious: As they approached him, he shouted at his daughter-in-law, "All I asked you to do was keep an eye on your daughter and you couldn't even do that! We cannot afford to give the soldiers an opportunity to question her . . . and you, young woman, could have gotten yourself raped!" Then, turning to Lilia, he warned her, "The next time you leave the house on your own, you are going to get spanked!"

Neither Maryanka nor Lilia responded to the grandfather. They were both terrified when he got angry.

When they entered the cottage, the grandfather gathered the women around him and told them, "Joseph and I decided it would be wise for the two of us to remain in our homes tonight, but it would be best for you women to spend the night in the cave. We have supplies and enough food stored in the cellar to last us for a while. All you need to take with you are your featherbeds and pillows.''

The Krameks' cottage and large barn were connected with a six-by-eight-foot anteroom, which had doors opening into the kitchen, the barn, and the backyard. The room's floor was built of wide oak boards with two square, equally spaced sections of inlaid woodwork forming geometric patterns. One of these squares was a hinged trapdoor hiding the secret entrance to the cellar below. The opening was large enough for a large man like Thomas Kramek to pass through easily.

That evening, immediately after the family had eaten their dinner, the grandfather opened the trapdoor and the women, one by one, went down the narrow ladder stairway into the cellar while he stood at the back door as a lookout for any soldiers coming towards the cottage. When the women were all safely down in the cellar, he followed them to unlock the heavy oak door that opened into a limestone tunnel, the entrance to the cave.

The basement cave of multitiered cellars of white limestone was a curious sight to Lilia. She soon explored every section of the cave and discovered a crevice in the limestone through which she could see the fires in the soldiers' camp. A heavy growth of blackthorn bushes and dense elderberry vines along the white loess escarpment hid the crevice from the outside, but the opening provided incoming fresh air and gave a clear view of the area from the inside.

The grandfather returned to the cottage, and the women retired for the night. Lilia snuggled up to her mother in the featherbed they shared atop a stack of straw. Overwrought by the excitement of the afternoon, she could not fall asleep. As soon as her mother was asleep, Lilia left the bed and walked down to the wall with the crevice she had discovered that evening.

Through the opening in the wall, Lilia looked out at the Russian encampment situated directly below the cemetery hill. She saw soldiers everywhere. Some were sleeping on the ground in the uniforms they had worn all day; others were sitting around campfires of flickering flames dying out. A few were hanging out laundry on the apple trees in the orchard. Where piles of dirt outlined the freshly dug trenches along the camp's perimeter the steel bayonets of the soldiers on guard glistened in the darkness.

Now and then, during a rare moment of silence, Lilia could hear the Vistula River rippling around its many bends and curves as it flowed between the hills of white limestone. In the full moonlight, she could see all the way to the top of the cemetery hill, where three wooden crosses were silhouetted against the sky—reminders of the many who had died during an eighteenth-century plague. Suddenly the moonlight exposed helmets bobbing up around the crosses. As they neared the ridge, they dropped low and slithered along the ridge like animals on their bellies. At the same time, wolves, hunting in the dark wooded ravine back of the cemetery, began to howl. It was all so scary. Frightened, Lilia ran back to her mother's bed. She crawled under the covers and pulled them over her head. Eventually she drifted off to sleep.

The next morning, as usual, the angelus bell at the local monastery rang out, calling the monks to prayer. It also awakened the Kramek family. Lilia jumped out of bed and headed for the secret lookout. The campfires were burning again, and black iron cauldrons, filled with steaming hot gruel, hung low over the flames. At each cauldron, soldiers lined up for breakfast. Lilia's eyes searched for Ivan. After some time, she spotted him standing in one of the breakfast lines.

Suddenly a roar of volley fire came down the cemetery hill, sounding like hell breaking loose. The shots came low and each met its target. Lilia saw Ivan fall. Caught completely by surprise, the Russian camp was in total confusion. Finally, one of the officers picked up his field glasses and looked up toward the hill. He shouted back to his men, "There are only a few up there! Let's go get 'em!" The Russians grabbed their rifles, with the attached bayonets and headed up the hill. At the same time, the Germans were descending. The two sides met in a bloody skirmish of hand-to-hand fighting. The Germans, on higher ground, had the advantage. Behind them, their reinforcements were arriving. The Russians retreated, leaving their dead where they fell. Among the dead lay the body of Lilia's newly adopted uncle, Ivan.

Maryanka was getting dressed when the volley fire came bursting close to the cave. Frances and Anna had returned to the cottage to prepare breakfast. The grandmother was still in her bed, just resting. Lilia was nowhere around, but Maryanka was not worried. She was sure that her daughter had left with the aunts and they were all hiding in the cellar.

It was the grandmother who noticed Lilia standing up against the stone wall a short distance from the sleeping area. She called out, "Maryanka, there is something wrong with Lilia!" and pointed to the wall where her granddaughter was standing.

Maryanka rushed up to her daughter and cried out, "Lilia, my child, what's wrong? Are you hurt?" She received no response. Lilia just stood there, like a stone, not moving an inch. The top of her forehead touched the wall; the palms of her hands covered her eyes. Her mother placed both hands on the little girl's shoulders and spun her around to face her. Still there was no response. Lilia's face was pale as the limestone wall behind her. Her big brown eyes, riveted

26

in terror, stared out at her mother. The gaping mouth uttered no words. With the help of Lilia's grandmother, Maryanka carried her daughter back to her bed.

Four days went by without Lilia speaking a word; then, on the morning of the fifth day, she called out to her mother in a weak, moanful voice, as if she was in great pain, "Mama!"

"Yes, my dear," her mother answered. "I'm right here."

"Is Uncle Stephen going to die?"

"We don't know, dear one. All we can do is pray to God that Stephen will be spared."

Maryanka realized she had given her daughter the wrong answer when she responded, "I don't like God anymore. He let the Germans kill Uncle Ivan." Then they threw their arms around each other and both cried. Lilia cried because she had lost her Uncle Ivan; Maryanka cried because somewhere in Russia a woman had lost her husband and two little girls would never see their daddy again.

While Thomas Kramek and his brother pondered what to do with all the dead Russians lying in their fields, a group of men arrived with wagons of lime. With the help of some Russian soldiers who had accompanied them, they stacked the bodies in piles on the sands along the river, poured the lime over the corpses, and cremated them.

Some days later, after all remains of the carnage were cleared away, Lilia and her mother returned to the cottage. In the days that followed the family came to realize what a severe emotional shock their little girl had suffered when she witnessed the battle through the crevice in the wall. The trauma affected Lilia deeply and brought about a great change in her personality. A strange sadness replaced the sparkle and alertness in her big brown eyes. The keen curiosity was gone. She had no interest in anything—she didn't want to play with other children. She refused to go with her mother to the market. The two black kittens, the brood of yellow baby chicks, the curly lambs in the barn, all had fascinated her in the past but now were just ignored. One night, she woke up the whole family screaming, "Uncle Stephen, Uncle Stephen, come back! They're going to kill you!" Every night, after dinner, the family prayed that this would pass and that the war would end.

The war in Eastern Europe centered in Poland, where the Russians fought both the German and Austrian armies, and brought the Polish people into direct contact with the conflict and all its horrors and hardships. In the beginning, the lines swayed back and forth with neither side gaining any permanent advantage but creating terrible destruction, chaos, and despair. While the village itself escaped the destruction inflicted on the surrounding areas, one of the water wells in the west section became contaminated and many young children and old people died of cholera.

As the war continued, shortages of food developed throughout the region and hunger ensued. There was great joy in the village when word came that donations of American food had arrived at the local markets. Grandfather Kramek remained in the cottage with Lilia and their big German shepherd to guard that none of their neighbors broke into their home and carried off what meager food supplies they had or even some of their livestock.

The four Kramek women walked the long distance to the marketplace, each hoping that she would receive a package of the donated food, perhaps some flour, sugar, rice, or other grain cereal. When they arrived at the market, the American food was there, but the merchants were selling it. Not only did they want money, but they were very selective as to what currency they accepted. Since that particular day the Russians were losing the war, the merchants did not want the rubles the women brought with them. They were only accepting the German marks. Disappointed, weary, and tired, the women returned home empty-handed.

During the winter of 1914–15 all was peaceful in the village on the Vistula River. Both sides had left to entrench for the winter. When the hostilities resumed, the Russian armies suffered great casualties. At the same time, a revolution was going on in their own country. The czar's monarchy collapsed, and the Bolsheviks seized power. The new government negotiated a peace with the Germans.

The Polish soldiers fighting alongside the Russians on the Eastern Front came home. The older Stephen returned; the teenager Victor did not. He was killed in the battle of the Mazurian Lakes, shortly before the poorly equipped and poorly fed army of 125,000 Russians was captured by the Germans.

Stephen rode to Lublin on a train bringing Russian troops home from various parts of the Eastern Front. From there he started out on foot for his home village. Twice he was able to pick up a sleigh ride from a peasant traveling the same road. Late in the afternoon on a cold December day in 1917, Stephen returned to the cottage on the Vistula River. Almost three and a half years had gone by since he left to fight in a bloody conflict the world will always remember as World War I.

Still wearing the Russian uniform of drab green with the high black leather boots, Stephen walked down the village road toward the family cottage. All along the way, dogs barked and growled at him and villagers watched through their windows, wondering what a lone Russian soldier was doing in their village. Those who had men in the service prayed that it might be one of their own coming home.

Thomas Kramek put on his coat and went out the anteroom door to see why the dogs were making such a fuss. He had barely opened the door when his German shepherd, now whining submissively, bolted through the opening and ran across the lawn, straight for the soldier. The dog jumped up with his front paws almost on the soldier's shoulders and tried to lick his face. The father knew one of his boys was home, but where was the other?

Frances and Anna were watching the soldier through one of the kitchen windows and witnessed the reunion of a dog with the man who had brought him home when he was just a puppy. Both dashed out the door to greet Stephen. Their mother followed them. Maryanka remained with Lilia, who stood at the other window, motionless and impassive, as if some little creature in her subconscious mind was whispering, *Don't get involved; don't get hurt again.*

When Stephen entered the house, Maryanka was startled to see how much he resembled his older brother, Adam. She longed for the husband she had not seen for six years and prayed that he, too, would be coming back soon to her and their little girl.

Lilia remained at the window. She turned around to face Stephen but made no contact with him. He ran up to her, picked her up off her feet, and said, "My, how you have grown! Such a little beauty, too. You won't need a big dowry to get yourself a husband."

For the first time in a great while, Lilia smiled, and she said, "Uncle Stephen, I missed you. I missed you a lot."

The pain of having to tell the family that Victor was dead gnawed at Stephen. Up to now, he had not been asked the question he dreaded to answer, but he saw it in the perplexed expressions on their faces and in their eyes. His father planned to talk with Stephen about Victor when the two could be alone. The mother could wait no longer.

"Stephen, do you know anything about Victor? Will he be coming home soon?"

Stephen pulled his chair up to his mother, took her hands in his, and told her, "Mama, Victor is not coming home. Victor is dead."

Agnes Kramek sat, stunned, but she did not cry. She had cried much during the years her sons were away, when the news coming from the war front was so horrifying. After a few moments, in a very weak voice, she asked, "Were you with your brother when he died?"

"No, we were separated at the time. Victor was in another unit," Stephen answered. He did not tell his mother that before the fatal day the Russian division to which the brothers were assigned had marched all week in extremely hot weather. Their food transport had been left behind. They were exhausted, starving, and surprised by a large German army coming at them. Two Russian corps were annihilated. Only about two thousand men escaped. Stephen was one of the survivors; Victor, who was ill from the hardships of the week, became an easy target for a German soldier in the swampy areas of the Mazurian Lakes region.

After a supper of sauerkraut soup with dried mushrooms, followed by poppy seed cake and tea, the family remained at the table. They exchanged their experiences during the war years and talked about the future, and they sipped on cherry cordial made from the fruit of their own orchard.

Maryanka retired for the night, taking Lilia with her, but neither could sleep. The small room off the kitchen had no doors. A heavy floral drape hung on a rod above the entrance and gave some privacy. It could not shut out the loud conversations in the kitchen, and every word was heard in the bedroom.

Stephen was heard asking the family, "Did you receive any letters from Adam after I left?"

"Not one," his father answered.

"Well, I do have some news of Adam, but it isn't recent. The day Victor and I reported for duty, we met Karol Mroz. He had come from America to visit his parents in Lublin. Since he wasn't yet an American citizen, he was conscripted into the Russian army before he could leave."

"He knew Adam?" the father asked before Stephen could say another word.

"Yes. They both lived in a Polish section of Detroit and had mutual friends. Karol told us that Adam was making good money in an automotive factory. He enjoyed living in America and had no intention of returning to Poland."

"I am not surprised," the father responded. "He will not be the first who promised to return and never came back. Remember Jan Wilk? After five years, he sent for his sons but not his wife. Stanley Nowak was another. He never came back and never sent for his wife or the children."

Frances joined in the conversation. "Both men had unhappy marriages. I do not believe Adam would abandon his family. He cared for Maryanka and adored Lilia. I am sure he will have them join him after the war is over."

"I think so, too," Stephen added, "but it may be a long time. The Allies are still engaged in heavy fighting with the Germans. Lord knows when it will all end."

The Kramek family sat around the table, sipping on the cherry cordial until all their emotional pain was gone. They then bid each other good night and went to bed. Maryanka and Lilia, having heard the conversation and the uncertainty of their future, cried themselves to sleep.

In the autumn of 1918, World War I came to an end. Poland, after a period of 123 years, became an independent country again.

Some time passed; still no word from Adam. Finally, a letter arrived and the news was jubilant. Lilia and her mother would be going to America as soon as Adam could make the necessary arrangements; but then a problem developed.

The U.S. Congress began setting up quotas and limiting the number of people who would be accepted from each foreign country. It became almost impossible for a person from Poland to come to the United States. More time passed. It was now 1919 and Lilia was still waiting for the father who was to have come home to her in the summer of 1914.

Lilia's father was a man with a warm, outgoing personality, who made friends easily. Not only did he have friends in the Detroit area, where he lived, but also among the Polish families living across the Detroit River in Windsor, Canada. One of his Canadian friends was Zygmunt Wrobel, an agent for the Canadian Navigation Company. Zygmunt made regular voyages on company ships to the Polish port of Gdansk to escort Polish families, coming to Canada for special land deals. He worked out a plan for Maryanka and Lilia to come to the United States through Canada.

On September 24, 1920, Lilia and her mother left the cottage on the Vistula River in Poland for the long journey to America. It was here that Maryanka, as a young bride, had come to live with her in-laws. It was here that Lilia had been born, the first grandchild of Thomas and Agnes Kramek. The family was elated that after nine difficult and tragic years their son Adam would be reunited with his wife and daughter, but it was a bittersweet day, too, for in their hearts all knew they would never see one another again.

Maryanka and Lilia took very few possessions with them. Both wore their best clothes—Maryanka, a black wool suit; Lilia, the brown velvet dress made by her Aunt Frances, considered by many the best seamstress in the village. Lilia also wore a strand of long coral beads, which had been in the family for many years. They were a gift from her grandmother. Among Maryanka and Lila's possessions was a brown leather bag with a complete change of clothing for each of them, Lilia's doll, and a tightly tied bundle, which was a newly made feather quilt. They had been told there were no feather quilts in America.

Accompanied by her grandfather and Uncle Stephen, Lilia and her mother left by wagon for Lublin. There they boarded the train that would take them to the port of Gdansk and the twenty-eight-day journey to America. When they disembarked in Gdansk, Agent Wrobel was waiting for them. He carried a copy of their passport picture and immediately recognized the young girl with the long braided hair and her mother.

"So you're the two pretty ladies Adam asked me to escort to America!"

Their faces broke out in smiles, and their eyes sparkled—something that had not happened in a long, long time. They followed the agent to a horse-driven carriage taking passengers to the ship anchored in the bay.

When they reached the ship, their documents were checked and they were given name tags with their destination to attach to their clothing. After their baggage was tagged, they proceeded down a steel stairway to the third-class section in the basement of the ship, called steerage. The large open dormitory had two separate sections of bunk beds—one for the women and the children, the other for men. Maryanka and Lilia were asked to leave their brown leather bag and the quilt in the baggage room, then were assigned their bunks.

For the next twenty days the bunks were their retreat from the cold northeasterly gales that rocked the ship as it sailed over the Baltic and North Seas and through narrow channels to the port of Liverpool on the Irish Sea. A ferry transported the passengers from the Canadian ship to the much larger SS *Corsican,* sailing that day from Liverpool, England, to Quebec, Canada.

Maryanka and Lilia left the meager accommodations of their ship and boarded the ferry with great expectations for a pleasant voyage for the remainder of their journey. The conditions they found were far from pleasant. Turning to a fellow passenger, Maryanka said, "I feel as if I've just left the suffering of purgatory and descended into the torments of hell."

"The torments of hell" was a fitting description for the steerage section, where conditions were appalling. The tossing and rocking of the *Corsican* in the giant Atlantic waves made passengers ill. Some were seasick; some had diarrhea. More than a few suffered from both curses. For the number of people crowded into the steerage area the toilet facilities were not adequate. The lines were long and the waiting miserable for those who were suffering with cramps or nausea. There were no facilities for bathing. Stale air and the stench of offensive odors made the steerage compartment uninhabitable, but where could the occupants go?

One afternoon, when the wild waters of the Atlantic looked extremely dangerous, Agent Wrobel came down from his second-class cabin to check on Maryanka and Lilia. A frail, middle-aged Italian man was down on his knees, his arms outstretched, praying loudly in his native language.

Maryanka suggested, "Perhaps we all should be down on our knees, praying to God that the ship doesn't sink and take us all to the bottom of the sea."

Agent Wrobel, who understood Italian, answered, "That is not what the man is praying for. He is begging God to sink the ship and end his agony."

Agent Wrobel looked after Lilia and her mother as he would his own family. He especially requested to be assigned a cabin near the stairway leading to the steerage section where they bunked. His frequent visits often included food sneaked out of the second-class dining room—a piece of meat rolled up in a slice of bread or a pastry for each of them. It helped to break the monotony of their steady diet of watered-down soup, boiled potatoes, and bread. Most of all, he was concerned that they not become ill. He had his own remedies, but would they work for them?

While the passengers from the Canadian ship were being transferred to the *Corsican,* Wrobel went into Liverpool to buy some black tea, lemons, and a large bag of English scones. He already had, in his trunk aboard ship, a bottle of Polish tonic, used for stomach ailments; a fifth of Canadian whiskey, a swig of which he added to a cup of tea with lemon juice; and a flask of French cognac that he enjoyed sipping after dinner. The soft scones dried out quickly, but when served with strong tea could lessen the severity of diarrhea or even prevent it. His recommendation for avoiding seasickness was, "Stay in your bunk. Lie flat on your back."

Either their mentor's remedies were really effective or both Lilia and her mother had strong physical constitutions. Neither of them suffered the miserable ailments afflicting so many of the passengers.

After what seemed like eternity, the *Corsican* left the death-threatening storms of the Atlantic Ocean and entered the Gulf of Saint Lawrence, then sailed up to the Saint Lawrence River to the fort of Quebec. After a journey of twenty-eight days, a Polish girl and her mother had arrived in America. With Agent Wrobel as their interpreter, they quickly passed their physical examinations and cleared through customs.

Lilia held onto her mother's hand tightly as they walked through the wide doors into the waiting room. A man sitting on a bench facing the doorway got up and walked toward them. He was a tall, slender man—blond and very handsome. Lilia released the grip on her mother's hand and ran into the outstretched arms of her daddy.

Bibliography

Davis, Norman. *God's Playground: History of Poland, Vols. 1 and 2.* New York: Columbia University Press, 1984.

Everett, Susanne. *World War I, An Illustrated History.* Chicago, New York, San Francisco: Rand McNally & Co., 1980.

Hartwig, Edward, and Eva Hartwig-Fijaikowska. *Kazimierz Dolny on the Vistula Wydawnictwo.* Sport I Turystyka: Warsaw, Poland: 1991.

Reeder, Colonel Red. *The Story of the First World War,* Eau Claire, WI: 1967., E. M. Halet, 1967.

The Wonderland of Knowledge, Vol. 12. "The Eastern Front.", Lake Bluff, IL: Publishers Production, 1958.

And from experiences as told to me by my mother and oldest sister, who lived in Kazimierz Dolny, Poland, during the First World War.

King of the Hill

Once we had a little dog named Sparky. His mother was a beagle, a handsome dog with the black, white, and tan markings typical of her breed. His father—no one knew. Sparky had a thick red, slightly curled coat and a bushy tail that he waved back and forth like a plume whenever he was pleased. It could be a tidbit from the dinner table or a pat on the head. His legs were short, his head like that of a Pekingese, with the short, flat black nose and big round brown eyes. His eyes were capable of showing disapproval with the haughtiest and most arrogant stare.

Every morning, rain or shine, sleet or snow, Sparky could be seen running up the narrow country road leading to the old stone church on the corner. Tall cedar trees with wide spreading branches surrounded the old church and provided shelter for a slew of cottontails in various sizes. As soon as Sparky reached the church, litters of rabbits came out from under the trees, twisting, turning, and leaping in all directions. After he had chased the rabbits around the church several times, he returned home to his blue bowl of dog food and small white bowl of milk. Sparky loved Milk Bones, and other doggie treats.

A neighbor driving by on his way to work one morning saw the little red dog chasing a fox out of our driveway down the road a distance and into the woods. A few days later, the neighbor saw Sparky riding on the back of a stray dog several times his size, yelping furiously. He renamed our dog King of the Hill.

For ten years the spunky little red dog reigned King of the Hill. He never wore a collar. He managed to slip out of every one we put on him. He would not be leashed. He chewed them all, even the fancy red leather harness with the gold nailheads. We never did figure out how he managed to get himself out of that harness. One day, accidentally, we locked him in the woodshed. He howled unmercifully until he was released. We finally gave up trying to confine him in any way. He ran the forty acres back of the house as free as the deer that roamed the fields and the birds that flew the skies. He was a happy dog.

Sparky was extremely territorial and had a ferocious bark when he felt threatened, but he also had different barks for his other moods. After a while, we learned to recognize them all. A gentle sporadic bark, with running around the garden, warned us that chickens were scratching in the vegetable beds. Sharper, more persistent barking usually meant cattle had broken through the fence and were feeding in a grain or hay field. A snake slithering in the grass, a squirrel robbing the bird feeder, or a raccoon raiding the corn patch brought out the worst in the little red dog. The barking was vicious.

He killed snakes by throwing them up in the air. The squirrels he chased up the first thing they could climb. They were seen scampering up the aluminum siding to the roof of the house and running to the very top of the telephone pole, each time just making it before they got caught by the tail.

One day, Sparky chased a skunk into the woodshed and kept the critter there for hours. Every time the skunk tried to leave, the dog blocked the doorway and sent him back into the shed. We had to fumigate the whole house.

When Sparky got into a fight with a family of raccoons, we all had to run to his rescue. He was no match for a raccoon, but we could never make him understand that.

One of Sparky's favorite pastimes was digging animals out of their burrows. He knew that a burrow had two entrances. He started the dirt flying at one entrance and quickly ran to the other hole just as the animal was trying to get away. The day he followed a woodchuck into his burrow in a large haystack, Sparky got himself in so deep he couldn't get out. We had to pull the haystack apart to save him.

Sparky was five years old when we took him to the veterinarian for the first time. He had been scratching and digging at his ears all week, and we decided to have the problem checked out. Doctor Morgan was the only veterinarian in the county. His clinic was near a large army base, where every family must have had either a dog or a cat. He had more business than he could handle. We left home an hour early, hoping to be among the first in line, but when we arrived there were eighteen dogs and three cats waiting for the clinic doors to open.

All was quiet as our car pulled up to the building. Every owner had his dog on a leash. Some were lined up in front of the entrance; others were walking around the large yard surrounding the clinic. There were poodles and spaniels, a red Pomeranian, a big black Labrador retriever, a long-legged Bouvier de Flandres, and others that were just plain dogs. Two cats were in carriers, a beautiful milk-white Persian and a black Angora. A little girl cradled a yellow kitten in her arms.

Before I could open the car doors, Sparky was already growling, running back and forth over the backseat, and scratching on the windows. He was ready to take on all twenty-one animals. As soon as we let Sparky out of the car, even though we had him on a leash, pandemonium broke loose. The dogs started barking, jumping up and down, and running around in circles, their masters desperately trying to control them. The cats growled, and the kitten spit and hissed. When the clinic doors opened, all were given a numbered black-and-white card and invited into the waiting room. We received card number twenty-two and were told to remain outside. We would be called when our turn came.

Sparky not only gave animals a hard time; he did not take too kindly to humans, either. All visitors, whether coming for the first time or having been at the house many times before, were met by the little red dog and kept at bay until one of us came out of the house; even then, he ran alongside the guests, watching every move they made. The neighbors' two boys frequently rode their bicycles by our house. Every time they passed the driveway, they hollered out, "Sparky is a bad dog! Sparky is a bad dog!" This affront sent Sparky down the road after the bicycles until he chased the boys back into their own yard, right up to the front door of their house. Then he scratched the ground under his feet a few times, sending the dirt flying up in the air as if to say, "Don't let me ever hear you call me a bad dog again!"

One summer day, a traveling salesman came around when no one was home. He made the mistake of knocking on the front door too many times and woke up the sleeping dog in the woodshed. The salesman left with strips of his pants remaining on our front porch and a leg wound that demanded the immediate attention of the local doctor. Sparky was picked up by the sheriff and taken to the county jail. Two weeks later, the sheriff reluctantly released the dog to my brother, Joey, with the warning that Sparky would be on probation for the rest of his life and if he ever bit anyone again, he would be shot.

Who would believe that this little red dog, so territorial and antisocial, was one of the most lovable dogs we ever owned? Four dogs preceded him, but not one was as loyal, obedient, and intelligent and gave us as much pleasure as

41

Sparky. We loved him dearly. He nibbled at our toes when he was hungry and nuzzled up to show affection. He was the only dog we ever had who liked to cuddle, but he was strictly a one-family dog. The family included Mother, Joey, me, and our three cats—a shining black female stray, who looked like a miniature panther, and her two offspring; a fawn-colored tom with dark-tipped ears, tail, and feet, whose father may have been a Siamese, and a black tom who looked just like his mother.

The three cats and Sparky slept in the woodshed, the dog in his kennel and the cats on top of the kennel on which lay a heavy wool quilt. Some days, Sparky and the cats all huddled together in the kennel. As soon as Mother walked into the kitchen in the morning, all four were waiting at the kitchen door, the cats scratching and the dog barking. While Mother prepared breakfast, the cats and Sparky wrestled on the kitchen floor. It was interesting watching them stalking and flipping one another over and over again. Sometimes Sparky got frustrated when he couldn't do some of the things the cats were capable of doing—climbing up a tree, jumping up on the windowsill, or sleeping on top of the wood pile, back of the woodshed, on a sunny day. No matter how hard he tried to climb or jump, all he succeeded in doing was scraping some bark off the tree or knocking a few logs off the wood pile.

For a number of years Sparky was an excellent herd dog, eagerly accompanying us to the forty-acre track of woods and pasture to bring the cows home for the evening milking. The wooded area had paths running in all directions but he knew exactly which path the cattle had taken when last they passed through the area. He located them very quickly, even though they may have been lying among the shoulder-high ferns.

The lead cow, Rosie, and Sparky had no love for each other. She was always the first one he got moving along. If she moved too slowly to suit him, he nudged her by pulling at her tail. She, in turn, tried to butt him with her horns. He was too fast for her and always jumped aside before she could touch him. One evening, he pulled at Rosie's tail once too often or, perhaps, too hard, and the cow took off at high speed with the little red dog hanging onto her tail for dear life. She ran around the barn, swinging him from side to side, and then flung him up in the air. He came crashing down to the ground. That was the last time we got any help from Sparky in bringing the cows home. No matter where he was or what he was doing, when it came time to bring the cows home, Sparky headed for the back porch. While we walked back and forth across the forty acres listening for the brassy clanging of a cow bell, Sparky took himself a good snooze.

Then there was the day, we gave Sparky his first bath. While Joey tried to hold Sparky down, I soaped and rinsed the heavy coat of curly red fur. As soon as Joey lifted him out of the tub, Sparky ran straight for the garden. He rolled over and over again among the rows of green cabbage plants. When his fur was completely covered with the black dirt, he returned to the back porch, where Joey and I were cleaning the tub. Standing defiantly before us, all four feet spread apart, Sparky gave us his most arrogant stare and let out a couple of angry barks. We understood—he didn't want any more baths. The next time he saw us bringing out the tub, he ran and hid far under the granary where he could not be reached. We gave up trying to bathe him. Whenever he got caught in a good rain shower, we dried out his fur with a heavy terry towel and fluffed it out with a good brushing. His favorite way of cleaning his fur was rolling across the living room rug.

During the ten years we had Sparky, I was teaching in a junior high school in Detroit, two hundred miles away from home. I always came home for the holidays and summer vacation. Once in a while, I drove up on a weekend. Mother said she always knew when my car turned off the main highway onto the country road that ran past the farmhouse. Sparky went wild. He ran out to the road and back to the house, jumped on the door, and barked, then ran out to the road again. Shortly, there I was, driving up to the front porch. As soon as I opened the door, he jumped up to greet me.

Two days before Christmas, the tenth year of Sparky's reign as King of the Hill, I left the city at noon and expected to be home, at the farm, by four-thirty. Snow had fallen during the early-morning hours, and I encountered long stretches of highway snow-covered and slippery. Driving was difficult and hazardous. It was seven o'clock and dark when I arrived at the farm house. The porch lights were on, but Sparky was nowhere to be seen nor did Joey come out to help me with the luggage. Two sharp taps on the horn brought Joey out of the house.

"Thank God you're here," he greeted me. "Mother and I worried about you all day." Then, he added, "We've got problems."

We carried the luggage into the kitchen, and as I entered the living room, where Mother was sitting in her rocking chair, I heard moaning. There was Sparky, wrapped in a blanket, lying on the braided rug in front of the fireplace. Joey had a fire going, and the birch logs crackled in flickering orange flames.

"My Lord, Joey, what happened to Sparky?" I asked.

Joey answered, "I think he was hit by a snowplow. When I came home from work, I found him lying up in the snowbank by the side of the driveway, shivering and moaning, his fur covered with blood and salt. No car could have thrown him up that high."

"Oh, Sparky dog!" I cried and patted him on the head. He wagged his tail. As I gently stroked his head, he let out a faint whimper and was gone. Joey picked up Sparky with the blanket and the rug and carried him out on the glassed-in back porch.

Joey told me that as soon as he brought Sparky into the house that afternoon, he immediately contacted Dr. Morgan, but the veterinarian had already closed his clinic. He would not come to the house, nor did he want Joey to bring Sparky to his residence. He told Joey that it was doubtful that Sparky would survive, but if he did, Joey could bring him to the clinic the next morning. We both felt that Dr. Morgan's refusal to give emergency aid to a badly injured little dog was cold and extremely cruel. I cried all evening and into the night.

On my way to bed that night, I paused on the landing at the top of the stairs and looked out the window to the north. A large lamp on the television antenna brightly lit up the area around the house. I saw dog tracks running in all directions—from the back porch to the orchard where deer came out at night to dig for apples under the snow; out to the granary and the barn where animals, from mice to woodchucks, had burrows under the wooden floors and the haymow; and all around the bird feeders from which Sparky chased squirrels all day long. From the bedroom window facing the south I looked out on the driveway and the country road. On the right side of the driveway, at the edge of the road, the snowplow had piled up a large snowbank. Here a little red dog and a snowplow had met that afternoon. The snowplow, with its wide steel blade, flung the little red dog to the very top of the snowbank.

The next morning, we had to decide what to do with

Sparky. Subzero temperatures had frozen the ground solid. No way could we dig a grave—not even with a pickax. In most places the ground was covered with at least two feet of snow; and where the winds piled it up high, the fields were impassable.

In the valley below the barn stood a large cedar grove. With snowshoes and a toboggan, it could be accessible. Joey found an old tool chest in the blacksmith shop. We lined the oak box with aluminum foil and placed Sparky with the blanket in the chest. Joey then nailed down the lid. We tied the chest to the toboggan and headed for the cedar grove. We found a spot in the grove that was free of snow. The branches were so dense that the snow was not able to penetrate and stayed on top of the branches. We laid the chest on the ground covered with dried cedar and covered it with green cedar boughs. Several rabbits were hopping under the trees.

Sparky's footprints haunted me all morning. No matter which window I looked out, there they were, running in all directions. By early afternoon, the snow began to fall again. It was a quiet day with no winds blowing, and the big flakes floated straight down from the sky like goose feathers. Soon they covered the ground and all traces of a lovable little red dog named Sparky, who was King of the Hill.

But for the Grace of God

When I walked into the township hall where the Alcoholics Anonymous meeting was held that evening, I didn't know what to expect. I had never attended an AA meeting. Ten people were in attendance. Two recognized me and waved "hello." Their expressions questioned why I was there. I was there because I had a story to tell—one I had wanted to share for a long time but kept putting off until this day. This is my story:

My name is Vickie Owens. I am not an alcoholic, but I could have been, and I shudder each time I am reminded how easily I could have been. I cannot remember exactly when I made the switch from sipping ginger ale to drinking alcoholic beverages. Long after all my friends were drinking beer, wine, and whiskey highballs, I was still drinking pop. One night, after sipping ginger ale from nine o'clock Saturday evening to one o'clock Sunday morning, I came home with such terrible cramps, I thought I would die.

The transition from pop to drinks spiked with alcohol came gradually. During the summer of my junior year in college, a school friend and I worked at the Wayne County Building in downtown Detroit. Every Friday after work, we stopped for dinner at Stouffer's Restaurant, which was known for its delicious food and "great whiskey sours." One day, Jean and I tried the drinks. From that day on, we had cocktails before dinner every Friday, and soon we were ordering two drinks before dinner. About the same time, I started drinking whiskey sours no matter when, where, or with whom I was "eating out."

After graduation from college, I rented a nice place in a private home. I had a large bedroom with an adjoining sitting room and study and a private bathroom. The rent also included kitchen privileges, and I made many of my meals during the week. On Sundays, I went to Aunt Mary's for the afternoon and Sunday dinner. My three cousins and I played cards and sipped whiskey highballs all afternoon. The girls drank their whiskey with water. I couldn't drink it with water, so they mixed mine with 7-Up.

The stores in downtown Detroit remained opened for Monday night shopping, and my cousin Julie and I often met after work, shopped for a while, then had dinner in one of the restaurants in the area. Julie liked a Manhattan before dinner, and I always had one, too. Sometimes Julie and I double-dated and went dancing to Polish clubs throughout the city. The clubs all had bars. Usually there was dancing for forty-five minutes, then a short intermission. We danced when the band played and drank whiskey highballs during the breaks.

There were weeks when I drank whiskey highballs on Saturday and Sunday, Manhattans on Monday, and whiskey sours on Friday. All my friends said they enjoyed my company much more when I drank than when I was sober. A few drinks would change me from a quiet lady with proper demeanor at all times to a good-time Vickie—talkative, gay, and witty—who would not hesitate to entertain her friends with a one-woman dance exhibition.

As much drinking as I did socially, I never drank at home. My landlady kept no liquor in her house, and I did not feel free to do so, either. But that changed when she sold her house and I moved into a place of my own. I had a beautifully furnished apartment and a well-stocked liquor cabinet, but I drank only when friends dropped in, never alone.

At that time, I was a home economics teacher in a very small school, kindergarten through grade nine, situated in a middle-class neighborhood. We had an all-white enrollment, teachers and administrators who had been in the building for a long time, and an active and cooperative Parent-Teacher Association. We had few discipline problems, and they were handled by the principal and her assistant.

After three years of evening classes and summer sessions, I received a master's degree in guidance and counseling and was promoted to a counseling position in a large inner-city high school.

My new school had an enrollment of twenty-five hundred students. Eighty percent were Afro-Americans. I had never worked with black students, and I had difficulty understanding their speech and recognizing their faces—they all looked the same to me. My counseling load was 400 students. I was responsible for all their scholastic and attendance records. The principal and assistants handled only the serious disciplinary problems. The rest were sent to the counselors.

One of my students, a heavyset, surly Rufus Jones, was sent out of one class or another almost every day. One day, he refused to leave the room when his teacher gave him a pass to report to me. He told his teacher, "I'm not afraid of Miss Owens. I'll grab her by the throat and squeeze her until her eyeballs pop out of her head."

The teacher reported the incident to me, and the next day I sent for Rufus, but he was not in any of his classes, nor was he at home. I reported the absence to the Attendance Department. That afternoon, one of the officers reported, "Miss Owens, your Rufus is sitting in jail."

"In jail? What's he doing there?"

"Police picked him up on suspicion of murder. They think Rufus may be responsible for the stabbing of the old man back of the school last weekend."

"God, have mercy on me," I prayed. The threats of the burly Rufus could be deadly.

We had a long faculty meeting after school. I came home completely exhausted, physically and mentally. I made myself a pitcher of whiskey sours—had two drinks before dinner, the remaining two after dinner, and went to bed.

I soon established a new routine. As soon as I walked into my apartment, I kicked off my shoes and headed for the liquor cabinet. I no longer needed a friend to drink with. I was drinking alone. How much I drank depended on how bad a day I had in school.

One Friday, as I was picking up my mail, I met my neighbor in the lobby.

"Vickie, would you like to have a Manhattan with me?" she asked.

"I sure would," I answered.

How much I drank that night I don't know. My neighbor never mentioned anything to me, but when I awoke Saturday morning I still had all my clothes on. I had only taken off my shoes. My purse, keys, and mail were on the dinette table. The mail was not opened. The steak I was planning to have for dinner the previous night was on the kitchen counter, uncooked. I remembered going into the woman's apartment for a drink. I remembered nothing after that. It was my first blackout.

I was slowly becoming acclimated to the school environment, and most of the students had accepted me as the replacement for their black male counselor. Several of my girls who were taking business courses volunteered their help during their free periods, rather than reporting to study halls. I now had two helpers for each period of the day. They were efficient workers and pleasant to have around. Without them, I might not have survived.

Although more comfortable in my new assignment, I was still unhappy about the distance I had to travel to work. I lived in the southwest section of the city. The school was located in the southeast area of town. Twice a day I traveled the eighteen miles on a busy expressway during the peak traffic hours.

One morning, a truck on one of the bridges above the expressway broke through the barrier, landed on top of a car traveling a short distance behind me, and killed the occupant. As soon as I got to school, I called my Personnel Department and requsted a transfer to a school in my neighborhood.

The transfer came through two weeks before school opened in September, but the assignment was for a school on the extreme east side of Detroit—only a short distance from the suburbs. I couldn't believe it! The news sent me to the liquor cabinet ten o'clock in the morning. After I calmed myself down with a couple of whiskey highballs, I got in my car and headed east.

I had no difficulty locating the school. The building was very close to the expressway. The janitorial staff was busy getting the classrooms ready for the new semester. None of the faculty members were present.

I introduced myself, and one of the janitors took me on a tour of the building. The school was spread out over a large area. It had initially been erected as an elementary school, and two large sections had been added on at different times. The newest addition had a beautiful large swimming pool. There was also a large auditorium and a library. Counseling suites were situated in various parts of the building. I liked what I saw and considered myself fortunate to have received the assignment. I spent the rest of the day looking for an apartment and found one only two miles from the school. I would be moving to the east side.

Even after moving to the east side, I continued attending the Friday night parties at the dance studio and an open bar. The drinks were included in the admission price. One Friday night, I drank too much. The studio supervisor and my friend Jean walked me to my car.

Jean admonished me, "Vickie, don't you take the expressway tonight; you go on Eight Mile Road! And call me as soon as you get home."

Both watched in disbelief as I pulled out of the parking lot and headed straight for the expressway.

I remembered going down the ramp into the expressway and the telephone ringing when I walked into my apartment. It was Jean. "Thank God you're home." She sighed in relief. I remembered nothing else. How I came home all the way from the west side on the expressway that night I don't know. How did I know to get off at the correct exit, to take the right streets, and make the right turns and end up in my own parking space in the lot? All I can say is, "My guardian angel was driving my car that night."

The next day, when I picked up the afternoon paper, a headline on the front page screamed at me: **WOMAN RAPED ON EXPRESSWAY**. We were both traveling the same route and about the same time of the night. We were going home after spending an evening socializing with friends. Her car was forced off the road by another car, and the driver raped her. The story gnawed at me the rest of the day—it could have been me.

The incident brought my Friday night partying to an abrupt end. A week later, I was sitting home, feeling sorry for myself and ready to drown my sorrows by drinking the evening away. A knock on my door brought me back from the liquor cabinet before I reached for the bottle. It was

Nellie Hanson, the middle-aged widow who lived across the hall from me. Every Friday night she and her two friends played three-handed pinochle. She asked if I would like to join them and make it a foursome. Pinochle was the game I played with my cousins on Sunday afternoon when I had dinner at Aunt Mary's. I was delighted to accept.

Nellie Hanson and her two friends did not drink. All three were sharp cardplayers. I realized very quickly, if I was to be one of their partners, I had better keep my wits about me. I did not drink on Fridays until the card games were over; then I would have one drink before I went to bed.

Every day on my way home from school, I drove by an Italian restaurant called Antonio's. On Wednesday from four to six, Antonio's had Happy Hour. They served two drinks for the price of one. I became a regular customer and my Wednesday night suppers were pepperoni pizza and rosé wine, two glasses before pizza and two after. I left the restaurant "feeling no pain."

It seemed that Nellie was always in the hallway when I came home on Wednesdays, picking up her mail or the newspaper. One day she said to me, "I see you've been to Antonio's again. How did you ever make it home in that heavy traffic?"

I shrugged it off with a laugh. "Guess my car knows its way home."

Nellie did not find my remark amusing. She shook her head and in her quiet voice said, "Vickie, we are all praying for you."

I didn't think I needed prayers, but what harm could they do?

At work, I seemed to function well. I was never tardy or absent. My student records were always in order. When the state auditors came for the annual examination of our student enrollment, mine was the first roll book they were given. I heard my principal say one day, "I know they will never find any errors in that one."

I was known as a perfectionist and a stickler for details, and some said I was my own worst enemy. Many a day I went home spent of all my energy.

Around the Christmas holidays, after attending several parties, I became ill with a cold. I was a long time getting over it, and even after that I still felt ill but couldn't figure out exactly what the problem was. Nellie suggested I see a doctor. I didn't have a doctor. She brought me her physician's phone number and stayed with me until I made an appointment.

Dr. Barrens was a brusque old man who bombarded me with one question after another. All I could tell him was, "I just don't feel well." He wrote down on his notepad: "GENERAL MALAISE." He never asked me if I drank. I felt he already had the information from his receptionist, who was Nellie's friend. I went through a battery of tests and X-rays. I was sent to other doctors for more tests. By the end of the second week, I was sorry I ever stepped into Dr. Barrens' office.

Then came the day of reckoning. The testing was completed, the results in. Dr. Barrens wanted to see me again. He was not in the least bit sympathetic when he told me I had high blood pressure, high cholesterol, and high liver damage. The doctor believed that alcohol was bad for every organ in the body, and he himself did not drink. I was cautioned how potentially addictive a drug alcohol could be, how it could seriously endanger my health, cause dramatic changes to my nervous system, and even lead to insanity or death. I was told to try to stop drinking altogether, but if I did continue, to do so only in moderation.

I had difficulty trying to drink in moderation. If I didn't have that first drink, I would be all right, but as soon as I had the drink, I could have a second and often a third. It didn't make any difference if I was drinking at home, in a restaurant, or partying with friends. After three months, I had to go for a checkup. The liver tests showed very little change, but there was a slight improvement.

Several times I tried not having any kind of alcoholic drink in the house for a week, then getting a bottle of wine to see if I could have only one drink before dinner and leave the rest alone. I could not. I already was a workaholic, and a danceaholic. Would I also become an alcoholic? I had come to a fork in my life. I could only take one road. The decision had to be made soon; no one could make it for me.

I was no stranger to the consequences of alcoholism. I had seen it in the tortured faces and broken-down bodies of the men and women I passed on the streets and skid row when I worked in downtown Detroit. I couldn't erase from my mind the vision of one of these women.

She was a five-foot bundle of skin and bones wrapped in a dirty old red print dress and a torn brown cardigan sweater. Her face was puffy and flushed; her eyes, downcast. The uncombed, matted mass of hair cried out for a shampoo. An unlit cigarette dangled out of the left corner of her mouth. She reeked of stale liquor and urine, which ran down her twisted, wrinkled stockings and into her cracked black leather pumps—a sickening sight that made my stomach churn.

As I hurried past her, she reached out with one hand and tugged at my jacket sleeve. She pushed her other hand, with the palm outstretched, towards me and in a weak voice said, "Please, coffee."

I pulled a dollar from my billfold and handed it to her, praying that she would buy herself a cup of coffee and a sweet roll and not spend it for a shot of whiskey.

I sat in my easy chair, my feet propped up on the ottoman, and fidgeted with the fingers of my right hand, which usually, at this time of day, held a glass of wine. The vision of the skid row woman wouldn't go away. I tried to read the paper; I turned on the television—still the vision would not go away. I went into the kitchen, opened the liquor cabinet, and pulled out the unopened bottle of wine. I uncorked it, poured the contents down the sink, and flung the emptied bottle into the trash bin. That was fourteen years ago.

My liver eventually healed. Not one test in the fourteen years has shown any damage, but to this day I cannot have a bottle of wine in the house and take just one drink. If I take that one drink, I will have a second and sometimes a third. It's a rare occasion when I come home with a bottle—usually when I am going to have company for dinner.

Once I played a game of chance and almost became an alcoholic. I know that drinking for me will always be a game of chance, because I fall into that group of "one in ten" for whom drinking can get out of control and the power to choose whether to stop or not is gone.

Oh, Lord, how easily I could have become an alcoholic, and it is only by the Grace of God that I am not an alcoholic today.

A Gift of Friendship

It was Sunday evening and Father still had not returned from his trip to northern Michigan, where he had gone to see an agent about buying a farm. Rudolph, our boarder, had recently bought a new Model-T Ford and volunteered to drive Father on the two-hundred-mile trip. They had left on Friday afternoon, right after they came home from work. "We'll be back Sunday, around suppertime," Father told us as he went out the door.

I spent most of Sunday afternoon at the living room window of our second-floor flat, looking out on the street below. From my lookout I could quickly spot the black Ford returning home. It was past my bedtime, and I was tired but determined to stay up until Father returned. I settled down in the big brown leather rocker, holding my favorite doll with the long blond curls and pink organdy dress. I was hoping Mother would let me stay up until Father arrived. Mother had other plans.

"Maria, it's time you were in bed!" she called out from the kitchen.

"But I don't want to go to bed," I protested. "I want to wait for Daddy."

Mother strutted into the living room in her usual authoritative manner and in her usual stern voice told me, "We don't know when Daddy will be home. It may be very late, and he's certainly not going to have time to fuss over you. He's going to have supper and go to bed. Daddy has to be up early for work tomorrow."

I hesitated getting out of my rocker and wasn't moving fast enough to suit Mother. She grabbed me by my arm and marched me toward the bedroom. "You get yourself to bed, young lady . . . and stay there till morning!" Mother was so impatient with me. I overheard her telling Father one day, "Karol, I just cannot cope with that child!"

I was in bed, but I could not fall asleep, and as soon as I heard voices I hopped out of bed and ran into the kitchen, shouting, "Daddy, Daddy!"

Father picked me up high in the air. He gave me a big hug and a kiss, then told me, "Marisha, I bought us a farm. This summer you are going to have an eighty-acre farm to explore and a little girl, your own age, to play with. Her name is Annie and she lives across the road from our farm."

Mother never permitted me to get up in the morning until after Father left for work. Her excuse was, "Father needs to eat his breakfast in peace."

But the morning after Father returned from the trip, I got up from my bed quietly and stood behind the kitchen door, listening in on my parents' conversation. They were discussing Annie.

"Tell me about the little girl who will be Maria's playmate," I heard Mother say.

Father answered, "She's the same age as our Maria; in fact, she was celebrating her sixth birthday on Sunday. Her mother invited Rudolph and me for Sunday dinner, followed by birthday cake and homemade ice cream. That's what made us so late getting back home."

"Is she precocious and rambunctious like our little hellion?" Mother asked.

"No, she may be the exact opposite. She's a gentle, quiet little girl with a freckled face and a shy smile—very obedient and respectful. I think she will be a very good influence on our Maria."

"What if it is our Maria who is an influence on Annie? Her parents will run us off the farm."

"I hope not. Annie is the youngest in a family of five boys. Both she and her mother are anxious to meet Maria."

From that day on, the farm was all my parents talked about. The plans were discussed over and over again. Finally, it was settled. We were moving Memorial Weekend, when Father got four days off from the Lincoln motor plant, where he worked in the Paint Department.

The news that we would be leaving Detroit was very upsetting. Oh, why did we have to move? And, of all places, to a farm? I lay awake nights thinking about it, often crying myself to sleep. During the day, I had to listen to Mother's scolding: "Stop your pouting! It's not going to do you any good."

I loved Detroit. There were so many places to visit, so much to see, so much to do. There were picnics on Belle Isle, rides and swings in the parks, and Charlie Chaplin movies at the Krammar Theater. There were streetcars to ride all around town and shop windows to peek in on Michigan Avenue. And there was Rosenberg's large department store, where Uncle Tony bought me the doll with the blond curls and pink organdy dress.

Detroit was a great place to live, and so was the big white house on Thirty-fifth Street. On summer evenings, I looked out over the porch railing on the neighborhood below. I knew exactly where the ice-cream man was at a given time and could see the Sunday night waffle wagon as soon as it turned into our street. The warm waffles sprinkled with powdered sugar were so good. Directly below our flat was the grocery store that was a front for the Blind Pig. The Blind Pig and the store were both operated by our landlord. Whenever I walked into the store with Mother, I was given candy or a cookie.

59

Moving day came, much too soon. Mother packed the smaller items all week, and now everything was ready to go. I stood on the porch and watched the long white van pull away from the big white house and leave Thirty-fifth Street. Father went with the movers. Mother and I were going with Rudolph in his black Ford.

When we left Detroit that warm spring morning in May, the sun was shining, robins scurried across green lawns, searching for worms; purple lilac bushes and redbud trees were in full bloom. We traveled the city streets under arches of stately green elm trees towards Telegraph Road, a main highway that took us out of the city and onto a highway going north. My eyes were no longer shedding tears. The tear ducts had run dry, but my heart was filled with sadness as I looked out the car window and watched a city fade away.

As we traveled north, the houses became fewer and far between. There was so much I had not seen before—big red barns, silos, toolsheds, chicken coops, and hog pens. There were small buildings, too, the milk houses, ice houses, and even outhouses. Herds of cattle and flocks of sheep grazed in green pastures. I saw farmers with horses working out in the fields.

We made rest stops as needed and lunched on ham sandwiches and pastries filled with strawberry jam. Finally, late that afternoon, Rudolph turned his Ford off the main highway onto a narrow, winding, dusty road. We rode over a bridge and up a steep hill to an old gray house As the car pulled into the yard, a large group of people, both adults and children, came toward us. When Mother saw all those people, she cried. The entire Polish community had come to welcome us.

There were men and boys dressed in blue denim bibbed overalls with suspender tops, and women and girls in dresses of checked gingham, plaid, and floral prints, some badly faded. Most of the children were barefooted. There was hugging and kissing among the adults; the children just stood and stared at us. Among the group stood a freckle-faced girl with long reddish blond hair wearing a blue-checked gingham dress. She looked to be about my age. This girl watched every move I made. I watched her, too, but was not interested in making any contact.

I was dressed in my city clothes—a new pink plaid dress with ruffles and a big pink bow in my hair. My white slippers with straps across the instep fastened down with round pearl buttons, and my long white stockings were spotlessly clean. I wanted nothing to do with the barefoot girl with dirty feet wearing an old faded dress.

The moving van was still there, but Father was nowhere to be seen. Rudolph took us through a side door into the big country kitchens. One of the movers told us Father was on the second floor, directing the placement of furniture. I immediately wanted to run up the stairs, but Mother held my hand and would not let me go.

When Father came downstairs, the first thing he said was, "Marisha, Annie's here. Did you meet her?"

"I saw her, but I don't like her. She doesn't wear shoes and she's got dirty feet."

Father laughed. "All farm children run around barefoot when the weather's warm. You'll be a barefoot girl yourself when summer comes."

"I won't! I won't!" I shouted in defiance.

"Now that's enough of that, Maria. You settle down. We're all tired."

Whenever Father called me Maria, I knew I had better behave.

The movers left for the city; our neighbors returned to their farms. It was milking time and they had chores to do.

Rudolph was out in the backyard, just looking around. Mother was interested in seeing the rest of the house.

Besides the kitchen with its large pantry, there was an even larger living room. The double French doors between the two rooms had stained-glass panels. One big bedroom was downstairs. Three smaller bedrooms were on the second floor. An attic extended across the top of the whole kitchen. The attic walls were papered with newsprint from World War I.

The kitchen, with a hot fire going in the cookstove, was quite cozy, but the rest of the rooms were cold and damp, with a musty odor about them. The house had not been occupied for three years. It did not have running water, only a small hand pump on the kitchen sink counter; it had no indoor plumbing and no electricity. We ate supper that night by the light of a kerosene lamp, which emitted very little light and lots of bad odor.

After dinner, Mother opened up the sofa in the living room for my bed. The day that brought my whole world down around me had come to an end. Weary with fatigue, distressed with discontent, I pulled the covers over my head to shut out the painful events and fell asleep.

When I awakened the next morning, it took a while for me to realize I was not in my cozy bed in the big white house on Thirty-fifth Street. The French doors were closed, but the rocking sounds from the big brown chair still came through. Curious, I got out of bed, slowly opened the doors, and peeked into the kitchen.

"Come on out, sleepyhead!" Mother called out, pointing to the rocker, "Annie is here to play with you."

There was Annie, sitting in my favorite chair, smiling at me. She had on the blue-checked gingham dress of the previous day, but her feet were not bare. She was wearing ankle-high white tennis shoes.

"You want to come over to my place?" she asked. "I have something I want to show you."

I looked at Mother and she nodded that it was all right for me to go. "But you must have your milk and cereal first," she said.

I had breakfast, got dressed, and walked across the road with Annie to her place. Annie lived in a large fieldstone house with a roofed white veranda on three sides. We walked around to the back of the house, into the woodshed.

On an old folded patchwork quilt a black cat was nursing three kittens. Two of the kittens were black like their mother. The third kitten had a coat of beautiful silver gray. His paws, tail, and face were a darker gray. "We think he's part Siamese," Annie told me. Annie picked up a piece of twine from the windowsill and dangled it over the kittens. All three jumped around and tried to grab the moving string with their little paws. When Annie sat down on a wooden crate and dangled the string over her knees, the kittens ran up her legs and into her lap. She picked up the gray one and handed him to me. "See how soft he is. Stroke his head. He likes that," she told me.

Suddenly the kitchen door opened and Annie's mother called to us, "Girls, come in for cookies!" The aroma of freshly baked sugar cookies escaped through the open door. It was very inviting. We returned the kittens to their mother and went into the house.

After the snack of strawberry Kool-Aid and cookies, I asked Annie, "You want to come to my place and see my doll?"

"Oh, yes!" she answered.

Mother, who expected I would be coming back with Annie, had unpacked the boxes that held my dolls and playthings. My four dolls were sitting on the sofa; my set of miniature china was laid out on my play table with the two matching chairs. A small carton with my coloring books and crayons lay on the floor near the sofa.

I showed Annie my dolls first. She was especially attracted to the doll in the pink organdy dress. *"Oh, she is so pretty. What's her name?"* she asked.

"She doesn't have a name," I answered.

"Let's name her Suzie," Annie said.

"OK," I answered, "You have any dolls?"

"Yes, I have one, but she is not as pretty as Susie."

I picked up the doll from the sofa and handed it to Annie. "Here, take Suzie; she's yours for keeps," I told her.

"But I can't keep her," Annie protested. "I didn't bring a gift for you."

Mother was in the living room and at this point entered the conversation. "Annie, you did bring Maria a gift. When you came to play with her this morning, you brought her a gift of friendship. It is a wonderful gift and one that Maria needs very much. No amount of money can buy it for her."

Annie returned home carrying Suzie with her. Annie's father made a little wooden rocker for the doll—a replica of the brown leather rocker in our country kitchen.

The freckle-faced barefoot girl whom I had greeted with disdain the first time I saw her became my first friend and my best friend. It was a close friendship, spanning through our elementary school days, when we walked to school together, sat across the aisle from each other, and shared out boxed lunches. We studied together after school. We exchanged valentines and Christmas gifts. We were inseparable.

In the summertime, we picked strawberries on the hillsides, blueberries on state lands, and blackberries along the fencerows of our farms. During the long winters, we skated on the large pond on our property and raced our sleds down the hills of neighboring farms.

Our friendship continued into the teen years and the big Depression. We always had plenty to eat, but we both worried that our parents would lose their farms. We learned to dance at the Saturday night dance at the Grange Hall . . . and we would be separated.

One Saturday night, Annie got interested in Alan, a boy who went to grade school with us but graduated three years ahead of us. Soon she and Alan became a steady twosome. I went back to the city and returned to school. The Depression ended. World War II came and ended. Annie married and had two sons and grandchildren. I remained single and worked in a city high school, counseling students. Separated by many miles, Annie and I kept in touch with letters, telephone calls, and occasional visits. Our friendship survived the distance and the years. We were sisters-in-friendship.

After forty-five years in the city, I retired and returned to the farm. When I drove up to the house, there was no one waiting to greet me—not even my parents. Both had passed away. Father had died of a heart attack and Mother of pneumonia. Each death was sudden and unexpected, leaving me with deep emotional wounds. The old farmhouse looked haunted.

I walked up to the front door, keys in hand, but to my surprise, the door was not locked. When I walked into the kitchen, a wonderful aroma greeted me. Freshly baked sugar cookies were cooling on a rack standing on the kitchen table. I looked around the kitchen. Sitting in the big brown leather rocker, near the French doors, was Suzie—the doll with the blond curls and pink organdy dress that I had given Annie over fifty-five years ago. The dress was faded, but the porcelain doll was in excellent condition.

A great sadness overcame me, and, in memory, I returned to the day when I moved from the city to a farm in northern Michigan. I saw a freckle-faced barefoot girl in a faded blue-checked gingham dress standing with a group of farm families waiting to welcome my parents and me. I saw Annie again, sitting in the kitchen rocker when she returned the next day with her gift of friendship.

Annie's friendship had eased the traumatic change from my exciting life in the city to the quiet country living of a farmer's daughter. Over the years, it had brought me much happiness and comfort when I needed it. Now it was reaching into my retirement years.

I heard the French doors open and saw Annie peeking into the kitchen. I ran toward her, and she clasped her arms around me.

"Oh, Maria, it is so good to have you home again!" Annie cried.

And I answered, "Annie, I am happy to be back where I belong."

Good-Bye, Ellie Kaye

The sun is rising in the east; in the west the moon is still in the sky, a fading gray crescent of the last quarter of the full moon. Doves gather under the bird feeder. Their mournful coos break the stillness of dawn. Two hours ago, I awakened from a bad dream. It is still haunting me.

I dreamt that Ellie Kaye and I were standing with a tour group in front of a hotel in France. We were waiting for a bus to take us to Paris, where we would board a Pan American jet returning to the United States. All of a sudden, I was alone, standing on a deserted beach facing the Atlantic Ocean. Giant green waves dashed against the shore. Puddles of muddy water were all around me. A lone seagull squawked in the sky as it flapped its white wings above me. Not a person or a cottage in sight. As I walked along the shore, I spotted wooden packing crates stacked together as if to form a shelter. An unkempt old woman in a ragged black coat walked out of the shelter and toward me.

"I got lost from my group," I said, stretching my arms out in desperation.

The woman looked me over suspiciously, then said, "Je ne comprends pas." She understood no English; I spoke no French.

In panic, I cried out, "Ellie, how could you leave me like this? Why did you not tell the guide I was missing?"

I heard a plane flying low overhead. I looked up toward the sky. It was a Pan American jet, number 125. It was the plane taking our tour group back home. I awoke.

I was drinking my morning coffee and reading the newspaper when the telephone rang. Earlier in the week, Ellie had called to tell me that we had an invitation to visit her niece Caroline, who had recently moved into a beautiful southern mansion in Richmond, Virginia. Caroline was the daughter of Ellie's sister Marian, and just as soon as a date was decided on I would be hearing from Marian, so I was not surprised when I picked up the phone to hear Marian's voice, but I was surprised to hear her say, "Maria, brace yourself, I am calling with some very bad news." She hesitated for a moment, then continued, "Ellie suffered a heart attack this morning. She called me shortly after four o'clock, said she wasn't feeling well and wanted me to come over right away. When I arrived at her house, she had already passed out. I called nine-one-one and the ambulance rushed her to the hospital, but the doctors were not able to revive her."

The news stunned me like a bolt of lightning out of the sky. Ellie gone? The vivacious, energetic Ellie, who never had a serious illness in her whole life. It couldn't be. Only three months ago, she had visited me at the farm. We went for a walk with my cocker spaniel and I could hardly keep up with Ellie.

Ellie Kaye and I were friends since childhood days. We were born in the same year—she in June, I in December. We were also related. Her mother and my father were cousins. Beyond that we were different as night and day. Ellie was an energetic, vivacious redhead, sometimes loud; always happy-go-lucky and outgoing. She loved to be surrounded by people and had many friends. As a secretary in an insurance office, when Ellie left work at the end of the day she was free.

I was her opposite—quiet, serious, reserved, and always going to school. If I wasn't doing research for a term paper, I was studying for an exam. As a teacher, I often brought home papers to check or worked on lesson plans, and as long as I had Ellie I didn't care to make any friends. I would not have time for them. In spite of our differences, there was a strong bond between us, and we did have two things in common. We both loved to travel, and we both loved to dance.

The year I was graduated from college, I did not take a summer job. I went home to the farm to rest up before reporting for my first teaching assignment. I had no money. That same year, Ellie inherited several thousand dollars from her godmother, who had married a wealthy man. The couple had no children, nor did the godmother have any close relatives left at the time of her death. Ellie's graduation gift to me was a trip to Europe. On a sunny day in July, we sailed from New York harbor on the majestic English ship the *Queen Mary*. We would be gone for twenty-eight days and visit England, Holland, Germany, Switzerland, and France.

The ocean was calm in July, and every morning, after breakfast Ellie and I strolled around the great wood deck of the elegant sleek red-and-black ship known as the Queen of the Seas. The wide expanse of the blue-green water surrounding the ship in all directions was an awesome sight. For four days the dining room served us meals fit for a king and stewards catered to our every whim. On the morning of the fifth day, we sailed with the morning tide into the English port of Southampton.

The port was swarming with activity—sailors hurrying home; baggage handlers sorting out the luggage; relatives, friends, and tour conductors milling around, watching the passengers disembark. Ellie and I cleared through customs quickly and had no difficulty locating our conductor with the large red AAA TOUR sign. John Burke, a tall, handsome Englishman with slightly graying hair, was a retired schoolteacher. He spoke all the languages of the countries we would be visiting and would be our escort for the entire trip. Mr. Burke had already purchased our tickets, and we immediately boarded the train for London.

The two-hour ride from Southampton to London took us through some beautiful English countryside. We saw many herds of cattle—Black Angus, red-and-white Herefords, fawn-colored Jerseys—and flocks of black-faced sheep grazing throughout the bright green pastures. Quaint cottages and magnificent manors along the way all had large gardens of flowers in various shades of red, yellow, blue, and purple, and all were in full bloom. Now and then an old castle popped up in the distance or we passed by a bombed-out shell of a building that had been hit by the Germans during World War II and was never rebuilt.

We arrived at Waterloo Station in midafternoon and were transferred by motorcoach to the Piccadilly Hotel. The building was old, the accommodations antiquated. Our bath water was only lukewarm. The chain on the water closet broke the first time we tried to flush the toilet. Just as we were beginning to worry that our luggage may have been left at Waterloo Station, the bellhop knocked on the door. We unpacked the luggage and dressed for dinner.

On the train ride from Southampton, we overheard a passenger mention that our hotel was situated in the Piccadilly Circus area. Since we were scheduled for a late dinner, we decided to take a stroll around the vicinity and look for the circus. During the four-day stay in London, we expected some free time and hoped to attend one of the performances.

I wore my kelly green print dress with the big red roses and full skirt and matching green high-heel pumps. Ellie had on her pale orange pin dot voile dress, which also had a full skirt and a large bow that tied under her chin. The straps of her high-heeled white sandals criss-crossed her slender ankles. Our skirts swished from side to side and the high heels clicked on the pavement as we walked briskly down the streets of Piccadilly. Walking the streets with us were sailors, soldiers, and a few civilian men. The women all seem to be standing on the corners or in front of buildings. Some of them wore heavy makeup and ornate dresses. Ellie and I had walked only a short distance when a sailor approached us and mumbled something We didn't stop. We just kept on walking.

"What did he say?" Ellie asked.

"I am not sure," I answered. "Sounded like, 'How much,' but how much for what?"

We noticed men approaching other women and engaging them in conversation; then the two would go off together. When we were approached for the third time, Ellie and I decided to return to the hotel.

On the way back to the hotel, we met one of the couples in our tour group. The man had been a navy officer during World War II and had been stationed in England. We told them about the activities we had observed on the street back of the hotel.

"You walked into a red-light district," the navy man told us. Then he laughed and said, "If you girls run out of money, you know what you can do."

"It wouldn't do us any good," I answered. "With our inexperience, they probably would threaten to kill us if we didn't give them back their money."

Ellie and I both came from very strict Polish Catholic homes. We had led very sheltered lives and were terribly naive about one of the world's oldest professions.

Our first full day in London was spent in a comprehensive motorcoach tour of the British metropolis. We visited

Madame Tussaud's Wax Museum, Trafalgar Square, the National Gallery, the Houses of Parliament, Westminster Abbey, Big Ben, London Bridge, the Tower of London, and Buckingham Palace, where we watched the colorful Changing of the Guard.

The second day of sightseeing took us through the peaceful Thames Valley to the Shakespeare country, including the historic city of Oxford; Stratford-upon-Avon, where Shakespeare was born; Shottery, site of Anne Hathaway's cottage; and Warwick Castle. We had lunch at a lovely teahouse that served delicious pastries. At every stop we were met by special guides who gave us a brief history of the place and pointed out interesting facts about the architecture, artworks, and furnishings. I was fascinated by it all, but at times Ellie seemed bored. What she really enjoyed was the evening get-togethers with our group in the pubs of London and the free time for shopping. Ellie was a compulsive shopper.

Our last day in London was a free day. We slept late, ate a continental breakfast of assorted rolls and coffee, then went shopping at Harrods. The big department store had a large selection of merchandise. We browsed through sections of beautiful bone china and crafted silver, soft woolens, colorful tweeds, and fine linens. Ellie bought cream-colored cashmere sweaters for herself, her three sisters, and her mother. I did not buy anything; I just looked.

In the evening, we were transferred by motorcoach to Liverpool Station and then a train to Harwich, where we boarded the cross-Channel steamer for an overnight journey to Hook of Holland. It was a journey neither one of us would ever forget. Heavy rain poured down on the steamer, huge waves of water dashed against the decks, and high winds rocked the boat from side to side. Fortunately, we had cabin accommodations. Some of the passengers did not. We jumped into bed, pulled the blankets over our heads, and huddled in fear. Would morning find us, two American tourists, arriving in Holland or two American corpses lying in a sunken boat at the bottom of the English Channel? We survived the stormy night and arrived in the morning at Hook of Holland, where a private motorcoach was waiting to take us to the Krasnapolsky Hotel in Amsterdam. We found the port of Amsterdam a fascinating place, laced by a network of fifty canals, spanned by five hundred bridges, and set against a network of fifty canals, spanned by five hundred bridges, and set against a background of windmills and tulips. The cleanliness of the city and the profusion of flowers in the windows and garden caught our eyes immediately. It was a most pleasant sight.

Shortly upon arrival at the hotel, we were served a luncheon of thick pea soup with spicy sausage, which the Dutch call *erwtensoep,* pickled herring, assorted cold cuts and breads, and sugared fritters for dessert—all served on Holland's blue-and-white Delft china. The afternoon was free. Exhausted from the stormy ride across the English Channel, Ellie and I slept the afternoon away. That evening at dinner, we learned that the night of our stormy crossing of the English Channel the Italian passenger liner *Andrea Doria* was struck by the Swedish-American liner *Stockholm* off Nantucket Island, Massachusetts. The *Andrea Doria* sank that morning.

The next day, immediately after breakfast, we toured Amsterdam, making stops at the Diamond Exchange, where valuable stones and industrial diamonds are cut; at the Queen's Palace; Rembrandt's birthplace; and the famous Rijksmuseum, which houses many of Rembrandt's pieces and a superb collection of Dutch and Flemish art. In the afternoon we went by motor launch through the canals, stopping at Volendam, where the fisherfolk still dress in their quaint Dutch costumes and wear wooden shoes. It was a delightful trip.

There was time for shopping, and Ellie brought along her large tote bag, which she was determined to fill up. As we browsed through the interesting shops, she bought Dutch dolls, shoes, pewter, and cheese. When we returned to the hotel, Ellie took the dolls and pewter out of the bag and placed them on top of the dresser with some clothes she had to repack in her suitcase. The bag with the cheese went into the closet.

The next morning, when I opened the closet door, the pungent odor of cheese almost knocked me over. Everything in the closet stunk to high heaven of Dutch cheese. We opened up the windows, then took the garments we planned to wear that day and started flappng the skirts, blouses, and undergarments in the outside breeze. A woman in the building across from our hotel was watching us and probably saying, "Two more crazy American tourists." Since we were unable to shake out the odor of cheese from our clothes, we spread them out on the bed and sprayed them with Ellie's Chantilly cologne. But that did not help; it just created a new odor. We got dressed and went for a walk around the hotel, hoping the smells would evaporate into the cool morning air.

The morning rush hour brought an outpouring of bicycles into the streets, far outnumbering the cars. Fearful of being run over by the bicycles, we returned to the hotel and entered the dining room for breakfast. Our group was already seated at the assigned table. We chose a table on the opposite end of the room, as far away from our group as possible.

When we returned to our room after breakfast, the question was what to do about the tote bag with the cheese? No way could Ellie take it on the bus. Both she and the cheese might get thrown off the bus and left by the wayside. For the chambermaid at the Piccadilly Hotel in London Ellie left a generous tip in American dollars—but when the Dutch maid walked into our room after we had left that morning she found a tan canvas tote bag. The bag was decorated with a brown design of two voracious white-ringed, bushy-tailed raccoons with black maskes across their eyes, staring out at her. In the bag were the souvenirs Ellie bought to take to her friends back home—ten small round balls of Dutch cheese, neatly wrapped in bright red and yellow aluminum foil and emitting a most foul odor. A note printed on a piece of white paper, with the hotel's letterhead, stated: "FOR THE MAID."

After breakfast, Ellie and I left Amsterdam by deluxe motorcoach for the journey to Koblenz, Germany; but before we left Holland we made one more stop—a visit to one of the great flower halls where millions of blooms, from roses and carnations to azaleas and zinnias, are sold at auction and shipped by air to all parts of the world. From there we proceeded on through Germany via Duisberg, Dusseldorf, and Cologne, the old cathedral city on the Rhine. We would stay overnight at Koblenz.

Our motorcoach driver was a German who spoke no English, but when he pulled off to the sides of the road, checked out the motor, and returned telling us, "Kaput," we all understood that we were not going anywhere for a while. The bus driver hailed down a truck driver and left with him. It was some time before our driver returned with another bus, and we lost a half-day of sightseeing. One of the sights we missed was the old cathedral in Cologne considered one of the largest and most important Gothic structures in the world. All we saw was its 515-foot spires in the distance.

The German city of Koblenz was 80 percent destroyed during World War II. The hotel was one of the few buildings that had survived the shelling by the Allies. Our room was on the side that had been bombed, and the outside wall was still missing. What once had been a hallway to the room was now an open balcony. The room was large, with a double bed and two commodes, one on each side of the bed. Each commode held a large floral porcelain chamber pot.

"They don't expect me to use that," Ellie blurted out in disapproval.

I did not intent to use mine, either, but, when we went down to the large public lavatory before retiring for the night we found the doors locked.

The next morning, we boarded a steamer for the ride down the Rhine River to Heidelberg. From the steamer Ellie and I watched the beautiful Rhineland scenery drift by. Each bend in the river brought into view another fascinating scene—castles perched atop terraced vineyards growing along the sunny slope; old fortresses rearing their battlements along the river and dominating ancient villages, walled cities, and deep moats; and cathedrals, some famous as far back as five centuries ago. Time had left its scars on them all, yet they seem to have been impervious to the modern warfare of World War II. We passed the legendary haunted rock the Lorelei, from which a siren was believed to lure men to their death. The summit of the rock, 132 meters above the Rhine, descends almost perpendicularly to the water, and its base has a sevenfold echo, which may have contributed to the rock's place in legend and poetry.

We left the steamer at Heidelberg and walked the narrow streets of the town, situated between picturesque hills covered with vineyards and forests. After visiting the university, Student Inn, and Student Prison, we rode on a cable car railway to a castle perched up high on the hill above the Neckar River. From there we viewed the famous Heidelberg Tun, a twenty-foot-high cask with a capacity of forty-nine thousand gallons. A stairway had been built on one of the tuns so that its top could be reached. That afternoon, on our way to Baden-Baden, we passed through the American and French occupation zones.

At Baden-Baden, one of Germany's internationally famous spas, we rested and relaxed amid beautiful surroundings, friendly people, and gracious hospitality, all the while listening to the ever-present German music on the air, most pleasant to our ears and stirring our dancing souls. The Germans made us feel that they were happy to have us visiting them. This was surprising to us, since only a few years ago we were bitter enemies.

Both Ellie and I were fascinated with the hotel's interior—the dazzling crystal chandeliers, beautiful oil painting, gilted walls and ceilings, ornate furniture, and the long marble stairway leading to a sunken tub, where we soaked our tired bodies before going to bed that night.

Our German meals were a royal surprise. We sipped wine from crystal goblets and feasted on delicious food. There was sausage, veal, pork, chicken, and fish, stuffed dumpings, cabbage cooked in wine, and salads sprinkled with cranberries. The rye bread was so crusty on the outside and so tender on the inside, I could have made a meal of just the bread and butter. For dessert we had ice cream, fancy tortes, and strudel. The rolls served for the continental breakfast were crusty and delicious, and for the first time since we left the *Queen Mary* the coffee was not only drinkable but also enjoyable. What a contrast these meals were to the greasy goose we were served for our first dinner in London, with more silverware than we knew what to do with, and the pickled herring we all refused to eat for breakfast in Holland.

Before we left Baden-Baden, Ellie went shopping. I just tagged along and browsed. Ellie bought beer steins for her friends who would have originally gotten the cheese she abandoned in Holland and a set of metal bookends—two knights in armor with all movable parts, a real conversation piece. The shop where Ellie bought the steins sent them directly to her address in the States, but the merchant in the metal shop had no such service. Ellie had to carry the box with the knights on the bus with her. There was not enough space left in the compartment above our seat for the box, so she placed it above the seat in front of us.

We had rotation seating on the bus, and this day the short bald-headed old man with the goatee was seated in front of us. For some reason, he had taken a dislike to Ellie. Her cheerful, loud exuberance seem to irritate him. As soon as the bus sped up on the highway, the box fell out of the compartment and hit the old man on the head, bounced off, and landed in the aisle. He jumped up from his seat, ranting and raving at Ellie. Such language as spouted from the man's mouth I had never heard before, nor is it fit to repeat in print. He demanded his seat be changed, but the driver had another idea. He took the package off the bus and stored it in the luggage compartment under the bus, where Ellie should have had it put in the first place.

On the road from Baden-Baden to Switzerland, we traveled through the Black Forest and more vineyards framed by snowcapped Alps. Strips of cultivated land gave the countryside a patchwork appearance. The pastures and fields of rye, wheat, and oats reminded me of our own Michigan farms, but there were fields of hemp, tobacco, and hops as well. We were surprised to see women working in the fields alongside the men and farm animals, from chickens to horses, housed in buildings annexed to the farmhouses.

In the afternoon we entered Switzerland and, after passing through Zurich, arrived in delightful Lucerne. Our hotel was situated in the heart of the Alps, and the view from our window was beautiful—a mirror-smooth lake with white-capped mountains in the background. We had a full day in this idyllic setting to enjoy the enchanting surroundings and shop. For the first time, I spent some of the money I had borrowed from Ellie for shopping before we left the States. I bought a small gold-plated fifteen-jewel Swiss alarm clock, an eighteen-carat gold ring with twenty-two cut garnet stones in a modern large-domed setting, and a carved music box that played my favorite song, *La Vie en Rose*.

The next day, the motorcoach took us for a thrilling ride on narrow winding roads over high mountain passes and through Alpine villages. All day long we traveled through the Alps. We gazed at the majestic towering peaks and the unbroken slopes, some covered with snow; others, with picturesque little farms and colorful houses. In the distance, we saw the spectacular scenery of the Matterhorn, the best-known mountain in the Alps, and the lofty Mont Blanc, the highest point in all of Europe. The height of the peaks was breathtaking; the narrow winding roads, frightening. With each approaching vehicle we prayed we would not be pushed off the road and sent rolling down the mountain to the very bottom of the slope.

Our journey took us via the Brunig Pass to Interlaken, located at the foot of the mighty Jungfrau Mountain, and through the spectacular Bernese Oberland route to the peaceful resort of Montreaux, where we stayed overnight. The next morning, after breakfast, we continued on a route along Lake Geneva to the city of Geneva, where we stopped for sightseeing.

The tour of Geneva included the International Labor Office, the Park and Museum of Ariana, and the buildings erected for the League of Nations and now used by the United Nations. We then proceeded on to Champagnole, France, passing through the Jura Mountains and stopping in Fontainebleau for a view of its magnificent palace, one of the largest of the royal residences of France. Our next stop would be Paris.

Along the road to Paris we passed by many a vineyard and one large beautiful field of lavender. We saw a man driving his horse and cart into a hay field and two women washing clothes in a river. Here and there we spotted storks with their long necks and beaks perched up high on a steeple or sitting atop a chimney of a gabled-roof house. There were small farms along the way with dairy cattle, pigs, and sheep. Our driver stopped alongside the road so we all could watch two large collies standing guard over a flock of sheep. The dogs lying at the edge of the pasture, their paws stretched out in front of them, their ears perked up, kept turning their heads in all directions.

As we entered Paris, one of the first sights to greet us was a large gray wall of graffiti telling us: "Yankee, Go Home." The slogan was extremely offensive to the World War II veterans in our tour group—especially one short red-headed fellow by the name of Scotty MacDonald from Chicago. Scotty was badly injured in Normandy. He had a brace on his right leg and wore a custom-made shoe with a built-up sole. He walked with a pronounced limp and carried a cane.

"Sons of bitches!" he yelled out. "We saved their asses in two wars and this is how they thank us?"

We arrived at the Hotel de Paris on the Rue de la Madeleine just before dinner The meal was disappointing and the waiters surly. Our travel brochures extolled French cooking as the best and most famous in the world. We expected Châteaubriand or a filet of steak, crêpes suzette, some fancy pastries. What was offered to us during our stay at the hotel was: tripe, sweetbreads, kidneys fried in champagne, goose livers, green oysters, meatballs made with fish, fish stews, and soup containing goose meat. Just reading the menu made me ill. We saw waiters carrying large platters of French pastries to other tables, but when it came time for our dessert they brought us canned pears.

The full day of sightseeing in the City of Light made up for all the disappointments we had endured since coming to Paris. Starting out with a walk on the famous thoroughfare the Champs Élysées, we strolled to the Arc de Triomphe. Beneath the arch, at the shrine of the unknown French soldier, we watched the flickering of the eternal flame for a few moments and offered a silent prayer. After making a short stop at Napoléon's Tomb, we continued on to the Eiffel Tower.

Standing on the observation platform at the top of the tower, 984 feet above the ground, we looked out on the Seine River with its many beautiful bridges. Suddenly the panorama of the city below unveiled before our eyes and we understood why Paris is referred to as the jewel of France. Before the day's end we visited the Cathedral of Notre Dame, standing on an island in the center of the Seine, and Sorbonne, one of the famous buildings of the University of Paris, stopped at a sidewalk café for French pastries and coffee, and walked through the Latin Quarter and up the narrow street and steps leading to the top of Montmarte, where we mingled with artists and poets. After stopping for a quiet period of reflection inside the Sacré-Coeur Church, we headed for the Louvre.

Formerly a royal palace, the Louvre is now one of the largest and finest museums in the world, housing many notable pieces of art and sculpture, both ancient and modern, among them the celebrated Mona Lisa and Venus de Milo. Returning to our hotel, we rode down the city's lovely boulevards, admiring the many beautiful gardens and other points of interest.

That evening, after an early dinner, we took a boat ride on the Seine River. Standing at the railing on the outside deck, we watched the scenery pass by. Artists could be seen all along the banks, some sitting, others standing at their easels, painting on their canvases. On the bridges above the Seine, booksellers tended their stalls. Then darkness fell on the city and all the lights went on. The Eiffel Tower, with all its lights aglow, sparkled like an enormous brooch with a with a million fine-cut diamonds.

Our last morning in Paris was spent at Versailles. There we browsed through the elaborate richly decorated apartments and the Gallery of Mirrors and strolled through the beautiful formal gardens with their many fountains. The remainder of the day was free, and we were "on our own" for lunch.

Ellie and I stopped at a sidewalk café, not far from our hotel, and ordered crêpes suzette. The thin pancakes filled with chicken in a rich sauce, were very good. We went all the way and also ordered French pastries. When the waiter brought us the bill, Ellie tried to pay him with American dollars. He refused to take the money. Then, she offered her American Express card. He wouldn't take that, either. We had already eaten the food, so it was more his problem than ours. The waiter became very angry. A tall distinguished-looking silver-haired gentleman sitting at the table near us was watching it all.

He came up to our table and asked, "What seems to be the problem?"

"He won't take our money," Ellie answered.

The gentleman picked up the bill from the table, looked at it, and paid the waiter in francs. Ellie offered to pay him in American money, but he declined, saying, "For two such pretty girls, it was a pleasure." He walked us to our hotel and told us he was from New York and in Paris on company business.

Shortly after our arrival in Paris, we discovered that our hotel had a hair salon. We made appointments to have our hair done on the last day of our stay in Paris, before leaving for Cherbourg. I was interested in a glamorous French hairdo; Ellie just wanted her hair cut. Upon entering the hotel, we went directly to the salon. I was taken immediately; Ellie was asked to take a seat and wait for the next available hairdresser. Patience was not one of Ellie's virtues. Before I got to the washbowl and turned around, Ellie was gone.

A few minutes later, an operator came to me and asked, "What happened to your friend?"

"I don't know," I answered. "She must have gone back to the room."

When I returned to our room, there was Ellie brushing and fussing with her hair. It had been cut. Puzzled, I asked, "Who cut your hair?"

She answered, "I did."

"I didn't know you could cut hair."

"I didn't either, but I know now. It doesn't look bad, does it?"

"No, it doesn't. I think it looks great." Ellie's hair was naturally wavy, and the shorter it was cut, the more it curled.

After dinner, we took in the early performance of the Folies, a theatrical revue of songs, dances, and skits. We were told that the sets and costumes were elaborate and colorful; the music and dancing, gay and delightful. No one told us the skits were naughty. Our eyeballs almost popped out of their sockets when the actors in the skit "Adam and Eve" came out on the stage stark naked.

Early the next morning, we boarded a special boat train for the four-hour journey to Cherbourg. The train traveled across terrain where American soldiers had fought during

World War II. All through the European trip I had always sat at the window and Ellie on the aisle. I liked to look out at the scenery, and Ellie like to visit across the aisle. But on this train ride, she wanted to sit at the window. As the train sped through the countryside, Ellie became very quiet. It just wasn't like her to sit so still and be so quiet. Then she reached into her purse and pulled out some Kleenex tissues. First came the tears, then the sobbing.

Ellie's only brother, Leonard, did not return from the war. He was one of the young men drafted and shipped off to England without as much as a weekend pass to visit his family before he left the States. At the time he was drafted into service, he was an engineer in one of the large automotive plants in Detroit and had a steady girlfriend whom he intended to marry. Perhaps he had a premonition he would not be returning. At the train station just before he left for Camp Custer, he told his father he didn't want his body brought back from overseas should he not survive.

To his girl he said, "Josie, do not sit around too long, against all hope, waiting for me to return. Find yourself a good guy and marry." But Josie waited five years before she even dated anyone else.

The telegram that Leonard was missing in action came before his last letter arrived The letter, written in London before D day, made no mention of the impending invasion. Some time later, he would be declared dead, but his family never received any information as to when and how he died—nothing from the government, no letter from a buddy or an officer, no message from a chaplain, nothing. They were left wondering; Was Leonard one of the GIs who struggled in the high-driven seas with a heavy pack on his shoulders and drowned before reaching shore? Was he among the men who were sealed in tanks that sank to the bottom of the ocean? Did he make it to shore, then was wounded

84

and lay among the dead when a tide came along and washed them all back into the sea? Perhaps he survived it all, only to be taken prisoner by the Germans and die in captivity.

Long after Ellie's mother was reconciled to the fact that her son would not be coming back, the agony of not knowing where and how he died gnawed at her mind and her heart and tortured her to the depths of her soul. When she died of a massive heart attack at age seventy, Ellie said, "My mother died of a broken heart."

Ellie had asked every veteran in our group where they were on D day and if, by chance, they may have met Leonard. None remembered meeting him. All were aware that Ellie had lost her only brother during the Normandy invasion. Ellie's sobbing brought Scotty MacDonald out of his seat. He asked me to exchange seats with him and sat down next to Ellie.

Putting his arms around her, he said, "Ellie, lay your head on my shoulder and cry your heart out, gal—you got to get it out of your system."

As the train continued on to Cherbourg, we enjoyed some picturesque scenery. One of the sights was Mont-Saint-Michel, sitting on the pinnacle of a steep rock like a crown—extraordinary, spectacular and dramatic. We finally arrived at the famous cross-channel port of Cherbourg, situated at the tip of the Normandy Peninsula. It had been the chief supply port for the Allied invasion of France. Here we saw great liners of other countries as well as many cross-Channel shuttle boats. The *Queen Elizabeth* had already arrived and was waiting for us. She was just as magnificent as her sister ship, the *Queen Mary*. We stood and watched until our luggage had cleared the gangplank.

We had free time on our hands, and the port had duty-free shops. It was a perfect combination for a compulsive shopper such as Ellie. I bought a bottle of Guerlain's Shalimar, which would become my favorite cologne of all time. Ellie got interested in the "special" on duty-free cartons of Courvoisier cognac, which was very expensive in the United States. Each carton contained four tall bottles of cognac, and only one carton was allowed duty-free per passenger. Ellie tried to talk me into buying a carton. Up to the time when I first started sipping wine before dinner in Germany, I had been a teetotaler. I did not want to be seen carrying a carton of cognac into the United States. Ellie bought the extra carton and put it in my name, and I got stuck with carrying it on the ship. I was very upset about it, but since Ellie had paid for my trip the least I could do for her was help her carry her booze back home.

When we sailed to Europe in July, the Atlantic Ocean was calm. Not one stormy day did we encounter. Coming back home in August was a different story. Although the *Elizabeth* was a newer ship and had stabilizers to help keep her from rolling, it did not keep the chairs and tables from flying into the air as far as their chains would release them. I spent most of the time in my bunk, lying flat on my back. Every time I tried to raise my head, my stomach started churning. Many passengers just stood on the decks, their heads hanging over the railing. For some reason, Ellie had very little discomfort.

After four days at sea, the voyage was over The *Elizabeth* anchored out in the ocean and waited for the U.S. customs officials to clear her for entrance into New York Harbor. It was a beautiful morning. Ellie and I stood on the deck, looking out at the shore and the city of New York. When we spotted the Statue of Liberty, we both cried. It had been a great trip and we enjoyed every day of it immensely, but after all was said and done, there still was no place in the world like the good old USA.

We got porters to carry our luggage to customs; the cartons of cognac we carried ourselves. We approached two customs officers standing together and set down the cartons in front of them. Big red letters running up the sides of the cartons spelled out: **COURVOISIER.** Smaller letters beneath the tile said: "Cognac."

One of the men turned and winked at his partner, then said, "Aha, two more cuckoo clocks."

As soon as we cleared customs, we hailed a cab and headed for Grand Central Station and the train that would take us home. In the years that followed there would be other trips. Some I took with Ellie; others, with teachers with whom I worked. None would ever compare to the trip Ellie gave me the year I graduated from college.

Besides traveling, Ellie and I both loved to dance. Detroit had several beautiful large ballrooms where the city's singles danced to the music of big-name bands. Then there was the Polish Century Club, which had dancing on Sunday nights with a Polish orchestra that played lively polkas and *obereks* in addition to regular dance music. On Tuesdays, we square-danced at the Campus Ballroom, a small hall not far from the apartment building in which I lived at the time. On summer Sunday afternoons, we picnicked in parks that had dance pavilions and polka music. Sunday nights, we danced away under the stars at the Walled Lake Casino with its large open dance floor and big bands. We spent our money on beautiful dance dresses and fancy shoes. Men thought we were wealthy women because we wore such expensive clothes.

From time to time we did date, often it was a double date, but it didn't take the men long to realize we had no interest in marriage, not even romancing—all we had on our minds was dancing. They dropped us like hot potatoes. One told me I wasn't the only pebble on the beach. Our egos never suffered, since by that time we had already tired of them anyway. In those days, my idea of a really great evening was to go to a public dance hall and dance every number with a different man.

Ellie and I used to treat each other to birthday dinners at some of the most elegant restaurants in the Detroit area. On her thirty-seventh birthday, we celebrated in a new restaurant that had just opened up in Northland Towers. It served delicious prime rib dinners and great whiskey sours and Manhattans.

As we sat there, chatting and sipping our drinks, Ellie sprang a bombshell. "Maria," she said, "I am going to get married. I want to have a family."

I sat there, stunned for a moment, then asked, "Who are you going to marry?" She wasn't even dating at the time.

"I don't know yet, but I'll find someone," she answered.

I almost choked on the piece of beef I had in my mouth. If she had said, "Maria, I've met this wonderful man and he has asked me to marry him," I would have been very happy for her, but telling me in such a definite tone that she was going to marry when she didn't even know who it would be just didn't set right with me. I was very upset. I ordered a second whiskey sour, which I had never done before.

Realizing that her remark had upset me, Ellie changed the conversation. "What time you leaving tomorrow?" she asked.

This had been my last day at school, and I was leaving for the farm the next morning. "As early as I can get myself together. I would like to get to the farm by noon," I answered.

We enjoyed the meal and had a good visit. I drove Ellie home, and in her usual cheerful voice she wished me a good summer and said she and her mother would drive up to the farm some weekend. They never came and I would not see Ellie again until September.

When I returned to the city, I immediately tried to get in touch with Ellie, but she was not home. Her mother answered the phone.

She recognized my voice and said, "Oh, Maria, I am so glad you are back. Maybe you can talk some sense into Ellie."

"What's happened?" I asked.

"She's gotten herself engaged to a DP!" she answered. "Maybe you know him. His name is Johnny Mazur. She met him at a dance at the Polish Century Club."

"No, I've never met him," I answered. I may have met the man but didn't remember him. After the war, many DPs came to the dances at the Polish veterans' club. They were the Polish soldiers, who had been stationed in England during the war and considered displaced persons after the war, since they could not return to their native land as long as the Communists were in power. Since these men had been part of the Polish army, they could end up being killed or imprisoned. Ellie's mother could not understand how Ellie could turn down a handsome American engineer who had graduated with her brother from the University of Michigan and whom she had known since elementary school and then get herself engaged to a man who didn't even have a steady job. As soon as the conversation was over, I dialed Marian, Ellie's sister.

Marian had married her boss, an elegant gentleman whose family came from England and whose father "dressed for dinner" every evening. She had been his secretary in a brokerage firm in downtown Detroit. Although much older than Marian, her husband was well accepted by the family and highly respected by all their friends. She lived in a big house in the suburbs and had three children, two handsome boys and a beautiful girl.

Marian told me that all of Ellie's friends were trying to talk her out of the marriage, but no one could get her to change her mind. When Ellie came home from shopping that evening, she called me.

It was after nine o'clock, and I greeted her with, "What did you do, run from store to store until they all locked their doors? What were you shopping for this time?"

She laughed and answered, "I was looking for a bridal gown. There's going to be a wedding."

"So I've been told. Have you set a date yet?"

To my surprise, she said, "Yes, January thirtieth."

"Ellie! A January thirtieth wedding in Michigan? We're apt to have one of those big snowstorms when you can't even get your car out of the garage."

She defended her choice of date, saying, "That was the earliest date available for the hall and orchestra that we wanted." They had chosen the Polish Century Club for their wedding and one of the most popular Polish orchestras in Detroit at the time.

Although Ellie had three sisters and many friends, some going back to elementary school days, she asked me to be her maid of honor. I was delighted. The day of the wedding, the temperature hovered near zero, but the sun was shinning. Ellie made a beautiful bride in her size 10 off-white satin gown with a long train and bodies of Alecon lace embroidered with seed pearls and a fingertip veil topped with a high crown of lace and more pearls. She walked down the aisle alone. Her father had died the previous year of a heart attack. The two bridesmaids and I followed her, wearing dresses of a delicate orange pink organza with full skirts and high jewel necklines.

All of Ellie's family, neighbors, and friends were there, 400 in all. The dinner was delicious, the music was great for dancing, and everyone had a wonderful time.

The first year after Ellie was married, I seldom saw her and it usually was at her mother's house when she had the family over for Sunday dinners. Aware that Johnny did not like me, I didn't feel free to just drop in on them. I always waited for an invitation from Ellie She continued working. Since I no longer had Ellie to "run around with," I was making new friends.

A year later, in February, Ellie had a son. He would be her only child. The day the baby was born, Ellie had gone shopping at a mall in the suburbs, twenty miles from her house. When Johnny returned from work that evening at seven o'clock, Ellie was not home. First he called her mother, then all three of her sisters, and last of all me. None of us knew where Ellie had gone, but we all told him, "She's shopping somewhere."

Ellie did not get home until after eight o'clock that evening, exhausted and complaining of abdominal cramps. She had gotten caught in the rush-hour traffic and there had also been an accident on the expressway, backing up the cars for miles and bringing all traffic to a stop. She had sat in her car for over an hour before the traffic began moving again. The baby boy was born that night. She was not expecting the baby until March.

To my surprise, I was asked to be the godmother; Johnny's brother was the godfather. They named the boy John Leonard. Ellie's mother was not enthusiastic about her new grandson. Whenever any of her friends inquired about the baby, she replied, "He's doing fine. Nothing wrong with him, except he looks just like his father."

After the baby was born, Ellie did not return to work. Johnny worked in a small precision tool shop and made good money, but he often worked long hours and came home late. My workday ended at 3:30, so I felt free to stop after work or visit with her and play with my godson. In the entrance leading from the driveway to their kitchen hung a tapestry with a homespun scene of a little white cottage centered in a colorful flower garden. Below the scene, embroidered in red floss, were the words "PEACE TO ALL WHO ENTER HERE." But it was far from peaceful in that house. Their little gray Schnauzer was always snapping and barking at someone or something, Johnny was hollering about one thing or another, and little Johnny was banging on his toys or tearing them apart.

Johnny doted on his little son, and the boy spent a lot of time with his father in the basement workshop. The child knew the names of many of the tools and the difference between a Phillips and a regular screwdriver. One day when Ellie and I were visiting in the living room, little Johnny was playing with the lower cupboard doors in the kitchen. A wide arch separated the two rooms, and I watched the boy take a Phillips screwdriver out of his toy chest and start unscrewing the lower cupboard doors. When some time went by and Ellie made no attempt to stop him, I couldn't stand it any longer and hollered at her, "Ellie! Your kid is taking down the cupboard doors."

She didn't even look to see what the boy was doing. She just brushed it off with a wave of the hand and said, "Oh, don't worry about it. Johnny will fix it when he gets home."

When Johnny came home, he was in a very bad mood. He had gone to work early that morning and had worked a long day. He also was having stomach problems again. The first thing he did was reach for the door of the cupboard where he kept his bottle of whiskey. The door flew off its hinges, as did the doors on each side of it.

"Stupid American builders!" he shouted. "They can't do anything right." Ellie made no attempt to tell her husband that it was not the fault of the builders; it was his son who was to blame.

From the very first time I visited the newlyweds at their apartment, Johnny was already having stomach problems. He often complained of heartburn and was treating himself with a tonic imported from Poland. Not until the problem became very serious did he make an appointment to see a doctor. The diagnosis was not good. Johnny had cancer. He had the necessary surgery, but weeks later he still was not able to return to work. The wounds were not healing, and he was losing weight. The doctor put him back in the hospital. Ellie said it was for more treatments. The next day, I went with her to see Johnny.

When we walked into the room, Johnny was alone. The bed next to his was empty. He appeared to be either sound asleep or in a coma. All kinds of tubing was attached to him. Ellie touched his hand and kissed him. He did not respond. When a nurse walked in, Ellie asked, "When is he going to start his treatments?"

"He's not scheduled for any treatments," the nurse answered.

"Why not?" Ellie said.

"The doctor didn't order any," the nurse replied.

"I want to see the doctor," Ellie demanded. "Will you get him for me, please?"

"I cannot do that. The doctor is not here."

"Where is he? " Ellie demanded again.

"He's on vacation in California," the nurse answered.

That did it. Ellie became very angry. "What kind of doctor would go to California without leaving the necessary orders for his patient's treatments? Aren't you people here going to do anything for my husband?"

By this time, the nurse also appeared angry. Unwittingly she blurted out, "Mrs. Mazur, there isn't anything anyone can do for your husband; his cancer is terminal."

The precise moment the word "terminal" left the nurses's lips, Johnny sat upright in bed. He took his two hands, grasped the tubing, and tore it all out, not only from his body but also from all the apparatus it had been attached to. What was in his left hand was flung to the left as far as it could go, and what was in his right hand went to the right. The nurse pressed the red light and ran out in the hall shouting for help.

Ellie screamed, "Johnny, please! Johnny, please!" and tried to get him to lie back in his bed.

Two orderlies rushed in and forced Johnny to lie down again. A doctor came in shortly and more nurses. Ellie and I were asked to leave the room. Ellie refused to go. The orderlies took us by the arms, and escorted us to the visitors' lounge at the end of the hall. One of the orderlies remained with us. Twice Ellie tried to leave the room. Both times the burly Oriental man stood in the doorway, his arms outstretched, blocking the exit. He reminded me of a karate instructor I had seen on a TV program earlier that week. After about an hour, a doctor came to speak with Ellie. He informed her that her husband's cancer had spread to the point where all they could do for him was give him medication to ease the pain and keep him calm. When we returned to Johnny's room, we found him heavily sedated and strapped in his bed. He died that night, leaving Ellie a fifty-year-old widow with a twelve-year-old son.

A month after the funeral, Ellie called to tell me she was going to work. She had not worked for over twelve years. The pastor of her church offered her the position of secretary-bookkeeper for the parish. She had been very active in the church's elementary school, which her son attended, and the Parish Women's Guild. Ellie was excited about the offer and looking forward to working again.

The parish of Saint Raphael had a large congregation, but there was a strong bond between the pastor and his flock and a closeness among the parishioners themselves such as I had never seen before. At the rectory, every day was open house, with people coming and going all day long. The kitchen counters were laden with all kinds of homemade goodies, fruits, and boxes of chocolate candy. All week long, Ellie nibbled on these goodies and even brought some home. The parish had many well-to-do families, and Ellie was frequently invited to dinner at some of the most elegant restaurants in the metropolitan area. Even after she retired, she was still being wined and dined by her friends, and the week before she died Ellie had gone out to dinner three times.

After my retirement from the school system, I returned to the farm, two hundred miles north of Detroit. Every fall, Ellie made the trip from the city to spend the first week in October with me. The color season in northern Michigan was at its peak at that time of the year, a panorama of brilliant colors, each species dressed in its own hue—the aspen and birch in yellow, the maples in shades of red and orange, and the oaks in deep rose and maroon red. Groves of green cedar, pine, and spruce intermingled with the colorful trees. Ellie and I hiked the trails through the woods, along the trout streams and the country roads. My little red cocker spaniel, Princie, went with us.

Just before Ellie's last visit to the farm, on the insistence of my doctor I had a complete physical examination. I was told I had high cholesterol. One morning, as we were walking down one of the country roads after a breakfast of scrambled eggs and sausage, which Ellie had brought from one of the Polish delicatessens in the city, the thought occurred to me that if I had high cholesterol there may be reason to believe that Ellie also had that problem. Her dietary lifestyle probably included more cholesterol in one day than I consumed in a week.

I told her about my physical and asked, "Ellie, when was the last time you had a physical examination?"

She laughed and answered, "I haven't been to a doctor since Johnny was born!"

"Don't you think you should see one? At least have your cholesterol and blood pressure checked."

"There's nothing wrong with me," she responded. "I'm as healthy as a horse."

The way she pranced down the country roads, neither Princie nor I could keep up with her. I was inclined to believe what she said was true.

The last day of Ellie's visit, we sat up late into the night reminiscing about events, some going as far back as our childhood days; others, as recent as our last trip, a cruise to the Mexican Riviera. As soon as we stopped laughing about one thing, one of us would remember something else and the laughter started all over again.

At the time when Ellie worked in the insurance office, her boss gave her two tickets to the Royal Ballet's performance of *Sleeping Beauty* at the Masonic temple in downtown Detroit. We got there early and entered a parking lot across from the temple. The parking attendant directed Ellie to park on the far end of the lot, up against a seven-foot-high stone block wall.

The tickets Ellie received from her boss were expensive, and we had excellent seats, facing the middle of the stage and in a row from which we could look straight out at the performers. Neither one of us had ever seen a ballet before. We sat during the first act watching the dances emphasizing the spectacular art of the ballerina, her partner jumping around in his skin-hugging tights, which showed off his male anatomy, and the mimed scenes unfolding the story through stylized gestures. Halfway through the act, just as I was getting fascinated with it all, Ellie began to fidget in her seat.

When intermission was announced, she said, "I've had enough of that woman strutting her stuff and the man showing off his thingamajig! He ought to be ashamed, wearing such tight pants."

She bolted from her seat and headed for the exit door, off the lobby, to the parking lot across the street. I followed her. The parking lot attendant was sitting in a small white gatehouse at the entrance of the lot, listening to his radio. He came out to meet us. Ellie handed him the parking ticket. "We're leaving," she told him.

The crotchety old man looked at the stub. His mouth flew open; his eyes stared at her for a few moments. Then he asked, "Woman, you crazy or what? You're parked against the wall. It's going to be a long time before you can go anywhere."

"I didn't park there by myself; you sent me there," Ellie retorted.

"Don't make no difference, lady; you're still not going anywhere. You a schoolteacher?" he asked.

"No!" Ellie shouted. "Why?"

"Because you look so mean," he answered.

I thought Ellie would say, "No, I am not, but she is," pointing to me. She didn't and I was glad.

We returned to the temple and climbed up the long flight of steps leading to the auditorium. The doors were locked on the outside. We took turn jiggling the door handles up and down and shouting, "Anyone there?" No one came to open the doors. The streets were empty and the whole area around the big building looked scary. I worried that we might get mugged. We ran back to the parking lot and sat in the car for the whole second act of *Sleeping Beauty,* listening to cats fighting in the alley, a dog barking in the neighborhood, and all the other noises of a big city on a Saturday night. I was so angry I didn't even want to talk with Ellie. What I wanted to do was kill her. When Ellie returned to work on Monday, she told her boss what had happened. He thought it was very funny. The tickets were given to him by a business associate, but he did not like ballet and never told his wife he had them.

During the cold Michigan winters, Ellie's favorite sleeping garb was a long flannel nightgown and knee-high wool socks. Her wedding day in January had been an extremely cold day. When she and Johnny went to their apartment after the wedding, they found it icy cold. Ellie insisted that Johnny drive her to her mother's place so she could pick up some of her flannel sleepwear. Instead of wearing the beautiful white silk gown she had in her trousseau, Ellie put on one of her old faded flannel nightgowns and a pair of knee-high wool socks. She had to threaten to return home to her mother before Johnny would stop laughing.

These were but two of the many episodes from past experiences that Ellie and I shared during our last visit together. Our long friendship was one of loyalty and companionship that brought us much happiness and, at times, gales of laughter. Now Ellie was gone and I was left with all the memories.

The church was filled with mourners. There were friends from elementary and high school days, the insurance company where she worked before her marriage, and neighborhoods where the family had lived and the parishioners of Saint Raphael's Parish. It seemed that once Ellie made a friend, they were friends for life.

In his eulogy, the pastor brought out her exuberant, outgoing personality, her cheerful, melodic voice, and her beautiful face with the perpetual smile. He said she brightened every room she entered and endeared herself to all who knew her.

We all gathered around the coffin in the cemetery chapel, bowing our heads, as the priest chanted the final prayers. My godson, Johnny, stood with me on his left, his wife on his right, tightly holding hands with both of us. His in-laws were all there, too. Johnny was an only child, but he had married into a large, closely knit family. They would take care of him. He would not be alone.

The family and a few friends were still in the chapel when two men came to get the coffin. I watched it being wheeled down a dark hallway. One of the men unlocked a side door and the other pushed the coffin into the room, and the doors locked permanently on a long and cherished friendship—*Good-bye, Ellie Kaye.*

Beyond the Summers, into the Sunset

Peter unfastened the chain from Moola's neck, and the cow scurried out of the barn, the last of the seven black-and-white Holsteins he had brought in for the evening milking. He closed the heavy wooden door behind him and found the other six cows standing around the building. Other times, they hurried to the creek as soon as they were released; today, not one moved from the barnyard area. Peter picked up the cane he kept outside the door and prodded the lead cow, Banna. She immediately headed for the pasture. The rest of the herd followed, one by one, down the hill toward the creek. Peter walked behind the cattle, his little white mongrel, Snowball, running at his side.

The sun was slowly moving toward the west, a blazing ball of orange with gold streaks radiating in all directions. A dark cloud hovered to the left of the setting sun. It was a quiet evening. Hardly a leaf fluttered on the small trees and bushes growing along the stream. Cat-o'-nine tails covered the marshy area, some six feet high with long cylindrical spikes of rich dark brown velvet. A mallard duck came out of the marsh with her brood of five ducklings waddling behind her in a disciplined line. The prescence of Peter and the little white dog did not disturb the duck family in the least. Peter watched each duckling dive into the water and marveled at the expertness with which the young ducklings swam.

The cattle were all drinking from the clear, cool stream, and Peter turned back, heading toward the hundred-year-old house on the hill. The Victorian building, with its long front porch and lavish gingerbread trim, carried an air of elegance about it. An orchard of apple, pear, and cherry trees framed the house on the north, east, and west. The large parlor window, facing the south, was filled with blooming pink geraniums.

This evening, in the cozy country kitchen, Peter's wife, Sophia, was cooking his favorite supper—breaded pork chops, scalloped potatoes, and apple pie. Peter had picked a basket of yellow transparent apples that morning. For him, no apple made a better pie than the transparent and no dessert a better finale for a meal than warm apple pie.

As Peter trudged slowly up the hill, his shoulders stooped and perspiration dripping down from under his old straw hat, he kept wiping his forehead with his right sleeve. Halfway home, he was greeted by a whiff of frying pork chops and the tantalizing aroma of the spicy apple pie Sophia had just taken out of the oven and set out on the windowsill to cool. Peter's steps quickened as he looked forward to sitting down to supper. Later he would relax in his black leather wing chair, resting his feet on the matching ottoman, while he smoked his corncob pipe and listened to his favorite radio program, *The Lone Ranger*. Often Snowball would be there, too, sometimes sleeping at Peter's feet, other times stretched out on his lap. It had been a long day from the time Old Red's crowing awakened him at five that morning. It was now almost eight o'clock.

With pleasant thoughts running through his head, Peter continued the walk toward the house. Suddenly he felt a painful crushing sensation in his chest It was the same pain he had experienced shortly after lunch. He was sweeping out the bins in the granary in preparation for the new crop of oats, wheat, and barley that would be coming through the threshing machine the next day. The pain lasted only a few minutes and was gone; but it left Peter very weak. He returned to the house, resting until milking time. Now the pain had returned, this time extending into his left shoulder and arm.

Along the path running from the creek to the barn stood two stumps, each a huge slab of pine wood, both relics left standing from the days when this was lumbering country. Peter staggered to the nearest stump, slumping down on the slab of wood. As he tried to prop himself into a sitting position, his left hand brushed against a bushy bull thistle growing alongside the stump. The plant, loaded with large purple blossoms, had dark green velvety leaves as prickly as the sharpest of needles. Instantaneously the hand recoiled.

Snowball came up to Peter and licked the sore hand. The dog whimpered and tried to climb into Peter's lap. Peter patted him gently and tried to push him down, but Snowball persisted With a long, mournful whine, he jumped up on the stump, and snuggled up to Peter, laying his head in his master's lap.

The cattle had all left the stream and gathered under the large sugar maple standing on the hill on the opposite side of the stream. Some were lying down, others standing. All were chewing their cuds. It was the first week of September and the crispness of a fall evening permeated the air, foretelling that summer would soon be over. Peter's pain was not as intense now, but he felt too weak to stand up. He watched screaming killdeer running across the meadow and the cows resting under the maple tree. The maple's green leaves of summer were turning a brilliant orange red.

Peter was not sorry to see summer's end. Summer meant long workdays, some stretching from sunrise to sunset. He was seventy years old, and the farm work was becoming more difficult for him each day. Two of his neighbors were retiring after the threshing season was over. Peter could not retire. He had no son to take over, not even a son-in-law. He and Sophia, his wife of forty-five years, had no children. Theirs was a small, not too profitable farm. They had not been able to save much for their old age. The small pensions they were receiving from Social Security were barely enough to take care of their meager needs. Then there were the taxes, insurance, and upkeep of a car that they could not be without. The nearest town was ten miles away, and each time they drove into town for groceries or church it meant a twenty-mile round-trip. No, Peter could not retire.

As Peter rested on the stump, barely able to sit up, scenes from his younger days came flashing before him. He saw himself again, a young soldier riding a chestnut Arabian mare on a country road in his native Poland. He had just received his discharge from the czar's cavalry in Russian Turkestan. Although Peter was Polish, southeastern Poland before World War I was under Russian domination and he had been called into military service along with the young Russian men. Now he was returning to his home village near the old city of Kazimierz Dolny on the Vistula River.

The three years of required service had passed quickly. He loved horses and was happy to have been assigned to the cavalry. As the time neared for his return to Poland, he began searching for a horse to ride home. He looked at many and rode them all before he found the young Arabian mare. She had enormous dark eyes and a silky coat of chestnut-colored hair. The skin under her hair was jet-black, giving her body protection against the rays of the sun and her coat its beautiful luster. The Polish word for chestnut being *kasztan,* Peter named the mare Kasztanka.

What a handsome pair they made as they rode along the narrow road to Kaszimierz Dolny: the delicate, slender chestnut mare with her arched neck and high-flung tail, moving in a graceful steady pace; the young man with dark brown hair and a handsome face, deeply tanned by daily exposure to the hot Turkestan sun. He was still wearing his cavalry uniform of a tan coat with the gray-green trousers tucked into knee-high shiny black leather boots. Peter sat on his horse, his six-foot frame erect and his head high, just as he did when reporting to his cavalry commander for inspection.

It was September and the trees along the sides of the road were arrayed in various shades of yellow, brown, and red. Peter especially admired the maples with their brilliant orange-red leaves. As they approached a heavily wooded area, Kasztanka let out two short snorts and slowed down her pace. Peter stopped and looked around. Sitting under a large maple tree was a small child. Peter dismounted and walked toward the child. The girl, about five years old, was sitting on a log, sobbing and wiping her runny nose with the hem of her red paisley skirt. She wore a white voile blouse trimmed with a multicolored floral design around the neck and sleeves. The girl was dark-skinned, with dark eyes and wavy black hair. She was a Gypsy girl. Peter stretched out his arms toward her, but she motioned him away, choking with sobs and crying out, "Lice! Lice!" As Peter came up closer to the girl, he saw small bluish patches of nits at the hairline above her ears. The whole head of hair seemed to be moving. He had seen cases of lice before but never a head of hair so infested with vermin. This was not a lost child but one the Gypsies had abandoned.

Peter's first thought was to take the girl with him. A short distance back, he had passed the mansion of the wealthy landowner Pan Jankowski. The forest area where the girl had been left abandoned belonged to the Pan's estate. Peter hoped to leave the girl with the servants. They would notify the village magistrate, and the Gypsies would be apprehended. But, just as quickly, another thought occurred to him. He remembered when one of his brothers came home with lice after playing with the children of a ne'er-do-well family in the village. How angry his mother had been! To have lice was a disgrace. If he took the girl with him, he would have to seat her in front of him and hold her close so that she would not fall off the horse. He could come home, a soldier from the czar's cavalry; infested with lice. He would be the laughingstock of the whole village! Peter told the girl to remain where she was and he would be back. He mounted his horse and galloped toward the mansion.

As Peter turned onto the long, narrow road leading to the entrance of the Jankowski mansion, the gatekeeper spotted the galloping horse and opened the large iron gates. Pan Jankowski was not in residence that day. He and his family had gone to Warsaw to visit relatives; however, his overseer was nearby. He had just returned to the stable, after being out in the fields giving instructions to the hired hands. He had not, as yet, unsaddled his horse and rode out to greet Peter and to check on the nature of his visit. Peter informed the two men of the problems. The overseer instructed the gatekeeper to send out a carriage for the girl immediately; he himself headed for the village to bring the magistrate.

Peter returned to the site where he had left the Gypsy girl. Again, as the mare approached the wooded area she became restless. She snorted and neighed and pranced, digging into the dirt road with her front feet. Peter quickly dismounted. Using his reins, he tied the mare to a nearby aspen. He feared if he left her free, she would run off. He hurried toward the spot where he had left the girl. She was not there. A piece of her torn white blouse lay near the log where she had been sitting. It was stained with blood.

Pulling his lance from its leather protector, Peter went searching for the child. He heard a commotion behind some bushes and found two gray wolves pulling at the girl's skirt, each in his own direction. Running up to the animals, Peter lashed out at them furiously, wounding one of them. Reluctantly the wolves let go of their prey, ran off a short distance, stood, and watched Peter. One of the wolves let out a loud mournful howl.

The Jankowski carriage arrived with two men, but neither would step outside the carriage. Both had heard the howling wolf. Peter picked up the unconscious girl. Blood streamed from her neck and arms where the wolves' sharp teeth had left deep puncture wounds. He carried her toward the carriage. The men brought out the two carriage blankets. One was placed on the backseat; the other, wrapped around the girl. Gently Peter placed the small, frail bleeding body on the seat. The carriage sped toward the iron gates. Peter followed, his head hanging low in remorse. He should never have left the girl alone. He should have taken her with him.

When the carriage arrived at the gate, the overseer and the village magistrate were already there. The gatekeeper and his wife, a kindly-looking elderly couple, were also waiting. The gatekeeper's wife had asked a house servant to check the trunks of children's clothing in the mansion's attic and bring something suitable for a five-year-old girl. The plans were to cut off the child's infested hair and burn it along with all her clothing. Her head would be thoroughly doused with kerosene; then, both the head and body scrubbed with strong soap and water as hot as the child could tolerate. The magistrate would then take the Gypsy girl back to the village with him. He had sent out a group of men to apprehend the Gypsies and force the caravan to return to the village. It had been seen passing through the village a few hours ago and could not have gone too far.

Peter stepped up into the carriage to bring out the girl. He stepped back, stunned. The girl was dead. With the exception of Peter, everyone standing around the carriage that day had known there were wolves in the densely wooded area nearby. The wolf population was increasing and their food supply getting scarce. There had been reports of attacks on cattle and sheep but not on any human. Perhaps the wolves had never encountered a human so small, so frail, and so accessible.

Peter leaned against his horse, resting his head on her saddle. He felt faint and nauseated. His former clean, crisp uniform was stained with blood; some had trickled down into his boots. There was blood on his hands, and his conscience screamed out at him. He realized Kasztanka had been warning him the first time they had entered the wooded area. It was not the child that was making her nervous; it was the wolves coming in for the attack. If he had not been so hasty in leaving, he may have spotted them. How thoughtless and foolish he had been. The lice, if indeed he had contacted them, could have been cured, his wounded pride healed, the humility forgotten, but nothing would ever bring back the little Gypsy girl. With darkness approaching, and too weary to continue his journey to Kazimierz Dolny, Peter accepted the overseer's invitation to stay overnight.

The overseer, Adam Nowicki, was a short, heavy-set man of fifty. His hair was graying and getting thin at the temples, but his handlebar mustache remained dark and heavy. Adam also had served in the cavalry, and he and Peter got on well right from the start. Among the many men working at the estate Adam was able to find Peter a change of clothing that fitted him quite well. The bloodstained uniform was put to soak in a wooden tub filled with cold water. Peter was taken to the mansion's large kitchen where the house servants and the overseer ate their meals.

The evening meal consisted of freshly baked dark bread, pickled herring, beet soup with sausage and hard-boiled eggs, babka, and tea. After the meal, the two men went up to Adam's small living quarters over the carriage house. Adam recently had lost his wife of twenty-five years and was still grieving. He kept bottles of cherry cordial on hand to ease his pain. He brought out one of the bottles to share with Peter. The two men sipped the cordial, reminisced about their cavalry days, and exchanged soldiers' tales of Catherine the Great. When the bottle was empty, they bid each other good night and went to bed.

When Peter awakened the next morning, Adam had already left. A bucket of warm water and a washbasin were standing on the small table near the bed, and the uniform was laid out on the chair. Peter examined the uniform. He could not believe what he saw. All the bloodstains were gone. The cold water and strong laundry soap had washed away the blood, but the deeply imbedded memories of the fatal day left Peter with mental scars that would remain to his dying day.

Peter had returned to his village and married his child-hood sweetheart, Sophia. His parents were not happy with the match. During the three years Peter served in the cavalry, they had hoped that Sophia would tire of waiting for his return and marry some other young man in the village. This did not happen.

Adalbert and Victoria Kozak had three sons. All three were handsome, intelligent young men. Peter was the youngest. The two older brothers married into nobility and left home to help oversee the large estates of their father-in-law. They had married sisters. Both wives were elegant, beautiful women with dark hair and eyes and beautiful complexion. Sophia was a slender, plain-looking blonde. Victoria Kozak did not see her new daughter-in-law as particularly pretty . . . and she had no dowry.

Sophia's parents could not afford to give her the kind of wedding the Kozaks' relatives and friends expected to attend. To save face, Peter's parents provided from their own larders the bountiful wedding feast. There was chicken soup with homemade noodles, sausage and sauerkraut, chicken, pork chops, new potatoes with dill, and various Polish pastries and cakes. The supply of drinks was generous, and the lively music was furnished by the best musicians in the area. It was a wedding that would be the talk of the village for weeks to come.

Peter's parents had expected their youngest son and his bride to make their home with them. Sophia would have been very happy to live near her own family, but Peter was restless. He wanted to go to America. The three sons and the father discussed the problem. It was decided that it would be best for all concerned if Peter was given his inheritance so that he and his bride could leave Poland.

Peter and Sophia came to the United States in 1912, first settling in the city of Detroit, where Peter found work in an automotive plant and Sophia in a glove factory. In 1920, they moved to the small farm in northern Michigan near the town of Alpena on Lake Huron. The area had a large Polish settlement, and two of the families were from Kazimierz Dolny.

In all those years, Peter had never told anyone about the Gypsy girl—not his mother, nor his father, not even Sophia. The first year they were married, he had frequent nightmares. On some mornings when they were having breakfast, Sophia tried to get Peter to talk about his restless nights. Once she told him that he had tossed all night, mumbling about wolves and Gypsy girls; another time, she heard him talking in his sleep to Catherine the Great and some guy named Adam.

Each time, Peter shrugged it off; saying he probably had a bad dream but didn't remember anything. After some time, the nightmares left, but the memories remained, and every September when the leaves on the maples turned a brilliant orange-red Peter relived a day on the road to Kazimierz Dolny.

Three hours had passed since Peter left the house and headed toward the barn for the evening milking. Sophia was becoming concerned. The supper was getting cold. What was keeping him? She walked out on the back porch and called out, "Peter Peter!" A whippoorwill, perching on the split rail fence at the edge of the woods, joined in the chorus.

Peter heard Sophia calling. He tried to stand up. The pain came back. It felt as if someone suddenly had pulled a heavy cord around his chest. He sat back down. There was the Gypsy girl, coming down the hill toward him. The two gray wolves were with her, escorting her, one on each side. They appeared to be very tame. As she came close to Peter, she stretched out both arms toward him. Again, he tried to stand up. His body reeled and he fell back. His left hand brushed against the prickly bull thistle. It did not recoil.

A slight wind had sprung up, blowing toward the west and gently moving the dark cloud until it caught up to the sun and now completely covered it. A slender woman, her silver hair pulled back and coiled into a bun, wearing a red-and-white gingham dress and a deeply worried look on her face, was running down the hill toward the creek. From the old pine stump, standing along the path to the creek, a frightened little white dog was running up the hill to meet her. From the distance towards the east came the wailing sounds of a freight train's whistle as it sped through the old ghost town of Alcona.

Vengeance Is Not Sweet

Lydia came running down the stairs from her flat to her mother's apartment. She pounded on the door, shouting, "Mother! Mother!"

It was six o'clock in the morning, and her mother was in bed, sound asleep. Lydia continued banging on the door and shouting louder and louder until she heard the door chain being lifted from its latch. The door swung open, and Lydia, standing in her nightgown, barefooted and sobbing uncontrollably, flung herself into her mother's arms.

"My Lord, Lydia, what's happened?" the startled mother asked.

"Michael didn't home home last night!"

"Did you call the bar?"

"Yes, he's not there. He locks up at two-thirty."

Lydia's mother placed her arm gently around her daughter's shoulder and led her into the apartment. 'Dear, I don't think that Michael would deliberately not come home. Something must have happened."

"Then why has he not called me?"

"He probably didn't want to wake up the boys. Let's call Josie. She'd be the last one to see him."

"Mother, Josie doesn't work there anymore," Lydia responded in exasperation. "He's got a new girl working for him, and I don't know her telephone number; I don't even know her name."

Lydia sat down at the small, round table in the breakfast nook and looked out on the street and driveway leading to

111

the backyard. Her mother plugged in the coffeepot and sliced some banana bread she had baked the previous afternoon.

"Mother, I think I should call the police."

"No, Lydia, wait a while. I have some concerns. If there is unpleasant news connected with Michael's absence, a call to the police may result in serious political consequences, especially since he is running for re-election. His opponent has friends in the police department."

"Oh, Mother, you're always thinking what's best for Michael! And while we're on the subject, I wish you would stop bragging about your wonderful son-in-law. Neighbors are referring to Michael as 'God's gift to a mother-in-law.' "

Michael O'Clery was a popular, charismatic politician. The tall, dark, handsome Irishman was president of the Springfield city council. He had a large following of prominent businessmen and citizens and wielded a great deal of power. As his wife, Lydia shared in Michael's limelight and prestige. She was expected to be at her husband's side at all important political functions. Lately she was finding her role more and more difficult. She no longer could keep up with the energetic politician in his campaigning.

Four months ago Lydia had suffered a miscarriage and lost the baby girl she had longed for. The loss of her baby had left Lydia extremely depressed. She was unable to shake off the melancholia. There were days when she could hardly make it out of bed to get her boys off to school. Mickey and Tommy, ages ten and twelve, were learning to shift for themselves.

Lydia drank a second cup of coffee, then returned to her apartment. Shortly after the boys left for school, Michael came home.

"Where have you been? I was worried sick about you!" Lydia shouted at her husband.

"You're always worried sick about something or another these days. I just had to have some quiet time to myself," Michael answered.

Michael showered, changed his clothes, and was leaving for the bar. When he opened the door, he turned around and faced Lydia. "I won't be coming home tonight," he told her.

"And just where are you planning to spend the night?" she demanded.

"I've set up temporary quarters in the storage room back of the bar. When I am reelected, I'll be moving out permanently."

"What about me and the boys?" she asked.

"Lydia, you're a liability to my career and a poor excuse for a mother," he answered in exasperation. "I want a divorce and I want the boys." Michael left the apartment, slamming the door behind him.

Lydia's mother watched Michael drive away and hurried upstairs to see her daughter. She found her distraught and in a state of shock. The news of Michael wanting a divorce and taking the boys was just as shocking for the mother.

"Mother, you won't believe how cocksure that SOB is! The election is weeks away; and to hear him talk, he's already won it."

"I can understand that. He's always won by such large margins."

"Well, he's not going to win this election. I'll see to that. I'll put him through such a scandal he will never get elected to office again. I'll get my revenge if it is the last thing I ever do."

Lydia's angry outburst and determination frightened her mother. "Dear, you must control your feelings. Remember, vengeance is not sweet," she cautioned her daughter.

"Oh, Mother, go back downstairs and leave me alone."

Reluctantly the mother returned to her apartment and immediately called her son, David, who was an attorney. She apprised him of all that had transpired that morning.

"I am not surprised," David told his mother. "I stopped at the bar last week and Michael told me that Lydia was just impossible to live with these days."

"David, we're going to have to get some psychiatric help for her. I am worried she may do something harmful to herself and the boys just to create a scandal for Michael."

"With the rumor I overheard the other day, Michael may be headed for a scandal on his own—he and Councilwoman Anders may be having an affair. So far, Michael's opponent has not gotten wind of it, but should the news leak out Michael is going to be in trouble."

"David, can you find a good doctor for Lydia?"

"I will try, Mother, but right now I have to leave for the courthouse. I have a case today. I'll stop by and have lunch with you as soon as the case is over."

As soon as her mother left the apartment, Lydia began to plan her revenge. Since Michael wanted the boys, her plan would have to include Mickey and Tommy.

Lydia turned on her kitchen radio and listened to the morning news and the weather report. High winds and severe thunderstorms were predicted for the afternoon along the Lake Huron area where the O'Clerys had a summer home. The weather report helped Lydia finalize her plan.

She quickly threw a few items into a large shopping bag and a bottle of sleeping pills into her purse. She wrote a short note to her mother and taped it on the outside of the apartment door, then quietly left the building without alerting her mother of her departure.

It was ten-thirty when Lydia arrived at the Springfield Elementary School. Since she was well known to the office staff, she had no difficulty getting the boys out of classes.

They were puzzled as to why they were leaving school but asked no questions.

When they were in the car, driving away from the school, Tommy, the older boy, asked, "Where are we going?"

"We're going to the lake. We'll have a picnic lunch and then go canoeing," his mother told him.

The boys enjoyed going to the big house on the shores of the Au Sable River, which feeds into Lake Huron. Both loved canoeing. Their father participated in the Au Sable canoe races every summer; and for the past two summers the boys experienced the joy of standing with a large cheering crowd watching their father paddle his canoe into first place.

It was the middle of the week, late in October, and when they arrived at the house the area was deserted. The day was hot and humid and very still, but ominous black clouds hovered over the land and the water.

The boys helped their mother get a fire going in the stone fireplace. They munched on potato chips and roasted wieners. Just before they finished eating, Lydia brought out a bottle of Squirt and poured the soda into three glasses into which she had dropped sleeping pills. She urged the boys to drink up quickly so they could get started on their trip.

The canoe sat on a low wheeled platform and rolled out of the garage easily. In a few minutes, they had it in the water. Although all was quiet when they arrived at their summer place, the storm predicted for that afternoon came suddenly and furiously. As Lydia was helping Mickey into the canoe, a streak of lighting flashed across the sky, loud thunder rumbled, then heavy rain came pouring down on them.

Mickey screamed in fear, "Mommy, I don't want to go!" Lydia tried to hold him down, but he screamed all the louder, "No! No! No!" He got away from his mother and ran back to the house. Tommy ran after him.

Dumbfounded, Lydia stood by the canoe. She watched the wild winds pick up milk cartons, tin cans, twigs, and papers along the shore and fling them all into the air. The winds pushed the canoe away from the shore, and high waves took it along with them and bashed it against the big white rocks across the river.

Drenched to her skin, Lydia returned to the house. Suddenly a great drowsiness overcame her and she barely made it to the sofa. She lay down and immediately fell into a deep sleep.

When Lydia awakened, the storm was over. It took her a while to realize that she was at the summer home and that the boys were there with her. The scene at the beach flashed before her eyes, and she jumped up from the sofa and ran into the boys' bedroom. She found the boys huddled together in Mickey's bed. Tommy had his arms around his younger brother. She tiptoed up to their bed and touched first Tommy, then Mickey. Their bodies were warm, and they were breathing quietly. Sighing in relief, she offered a silent prayer of thanksgiving as she realized that the sudden onset of the storm had saved her and her boys from a fatal revenge.

The long nap had refreshed Lydia's mind, body, and spirit. She walked out on the porch facing the river and sat down in the swing. The dark clouds were gone. They had been replaced by a beautiful rainbow. The arch of soft pastel colors—orange, yellow, green, blue, and violet—formed a frame for a landscape of white cottages standing on a hillside across the river. The waters from the heavy rain had rushed out to Lake Huron, and the river was flowing gently again. A white-tailed doe and her two fawns came out on the lawn to feed on the short green grass. Surrounded by tranquility,

Lydia was at peace again with herself and the world around her.

Swaying back and forth in the swing, Lydia pondered about her future. Before she married Michael, she was a legal secretary in her brother's law firm. She had stopped working when Tommy was born. Twice David had asked her if she would like to return to work; but each time Michael refused to let her go. She wondered if her boys would ever trust her again. "A poor excuse for a mother," Michael had called her that morning.

As Lydia sat there, alone with her thoughts, she saw her brother's white Cadillac coming down the gravel road around the bend. She knew her mother would be with him. With two strong allies at her side, she was ready to meet the future, whatever it would bring. For the first time in months, she felt life was worth living and was convinced vengeance is not sweet.

A Tale of Puppy Love

I fell in love with him the moment I saw him—the little red dog, sleeping in his cage, in a puppy mill. As I stood there, in front of the cage watching him, he became aware of my presence and raised his head. Slowly and hesitantly, he came toward me. I extended my fingers through one of the spaces around the steel bars of the cage door. There was a sadness about him as he looked up at me with his big brown eyes. I felt he was telling me, *Please, please, take me home with you.*

As the puppy and I were getting acquainted, an attendant walked up to me. "You interested in the dog?" he asked.

"I may be," I replied. "I am looking for a little dog for my mother. She is ninety years old, and I want to be sure I get her a small dog and not some breed that will grow into a hundred-and-fifty pound animal that she can't handle."

"You're looking at the right dog, lady. This one is a cocker–fox terrier mix. He's gonna stay a small dog."

"How old is he?" I asked.

"He's three months old. That's a good time to take a dog into a new home. You can take him home with you today—costs only twenty dollars."

"I want the dog, but I can't take it with me today. I live in an apartment where dogs are not permitted I'll have to wait until Friday noon, when school is out for the summer. I'll pick him up on my way to the farm."

"That's ok, but it will cost seven dollars more to keep him for the week. You have to pay it all now."

I paid the man the twenty-seven dollars, but I walked out angry. What if I had not bought the puppy and no one else did, either? The man might have ended up having to feed the dog longer than an additional week.

When I returned Friday to pick up the puppy, he was waiting for me at the cage door, wagging his tail. I had brought a little brown leather collar and a matching leash, and the attendant put them on for me. The puppy followed me down the hall and out to my car. He never looked back. I placed him in his new carrier, and we were on our way to the farm in northern Michigan, two hundred miles away.

I had to make several stops along the roadside to walk the puppy and made one stop at a roadside park where I ate my ham sandwich and he had his puppy chow. Tourists who were in the park at the time stopped to tell me, "What a cute little dog!" Some wanted to know his breed, and one asked, "What's his name?" Up to this time, I had given no thought as to his name, but now I looked at his rust-colored coat and answered, "His name is Rusty."

Rusty and I arrived at the farm at six-thirty that evening. My brother, Joey, heard the car coming into the driveway and was standing on the front porch, waiting to greet us. "What have we got here?" he asked when I let the little dog loose and he ran straight to the porch and the dish of cat food.

"We got ourselves another dog. Doesn't he remind you of Sparky when we first brought him home?"

"Sure does. That should make Mother happy."

Sparky, our last dog, had died on Christmas Eve after being hit by a snowplow. For ten years he had kept Mother company during the long days when Joey was at work and she was home alone. The little dog was a faithful, loving companion, and Mother missed him terribly.

Mother was elated when I set Rusty on her lap; but he got too rambunctious and she couldn't control him. He quickly became too much for her to cope with—he nipped at her heels, pulled at her dress hems, and chewed up her favorite slippers. When he pulled at her bathrobe ties and tripped her, Joey threw him out of the house and into the woodshed.

Not only did Rusty give Mother a hard time; he scared off our two cats. When I arrived home with the puppy, the cats were nowhere around. They came home some time later and found their food dish empty. Both scratched on the front door to come into the house. As I opened the door, Rusty came running from the living room with a wild, loud, *Woof! Woof! Woof!* Both cats hissed and spit at the puppy; and the big tomcat, Blackie, swung one paw and then the other across the little dog's nose. Both cats took off. Blackie came back home three days later, but Tiger never returned. He found himself a new home at a neighboring farm, where there were no puppies.

Rusty was confined to the woodshed and the area around it. Joey ran a long steel line from the shed out into the yard and fastened it around a strong bough of the big maple tree in the front yard. Rusty had plenty of room to run around it.

The type of close bond that had existed between Mother and Sparky never developed with Rusty. She would have nothing to do with him. It was up to me to give the puppy the attention he needed. I fed him, brushed his fur, and took him on long walks down country roads and into the woods back of the house.

One day, as Rusty and I were strolling through the woods toward the river, he got really excited and started yelping. I could hardly hang onto his leash. He had spotted a big black animal walking along the river. I retreated toward

120

the house as fast as I could run, pulling my dog behind me. He balked all the way. He wanted to run in the opposite direction—toward the river and the animal.

"We have a bear in the woods," I told Joey when he came home from work.

He laughed. "That was no bear you saw. It was Smokey, the neighbor's black lab."

"If he is the neighbor's dog, what's he doing in our woods?"

"He's a wanderer. Runs the whole section."

"The whole section? That's six hundred and forty acres! He doesn't get lost?"

"Evidently not. He's always sleeping on their front porch when I drive by in the morning."

"If he is such a rover, it seems to me that he should be penned up in some enclosure or leashed."

"He's a strong dog. He'd break loose from a leash and dig himself out of any pen. There are many dogs around here. Some farmers have two dogs. I haven't seen any of them confined. They all run loose."

The next morning, when I went out to the shed to feed Rusty he was nowhere to be seen. He had slipped out of his collar and disappeared. I walked out to the road, and there he was, running up the hill with Smoky towards the neighbors' house. I picked up Rusty's leash and went after him. There was no one home at the neighbors'. Both worked in town. I tried to grab Rusty, but he took off. The two dogs took me on a merry chase around the farmhouse, the big barn, and several smaller buildings. They had themselves a ball. I finally caught up with Rusty and walked him home.

I tightened the puppy's collar, and Joey shortened Rusty's running line so he could not venture out too far from the shed. We both kept a close watch on him, but we were never able to break up the friendship that sprang up

121

between the little red puppy and the old big black Lab. Smoky visited often, and when he came Rusty wagged his tail and leaped for joy. When the Lab left, Rusty whined and wanted to go with him. There was some physical force that drew the two dogs together. They would not be separated.

A week later, I returned to the city. I did not return to the farm until the color season in October, then again for Thanksgiving and Christmas. Each time, Rusty was not home when I arrived He was running with Smoky.

By Christmastime, I was very upset about the situation and confronted Joey. "Why are you allowing Rusty to run wild? He's going to get shot by some deer hunter in the woods or run down by a car on the road."

"Believe me, I have tried to put a stop to it. I locked him in the shed. He dug himself out. I piled wood along the wall so he couldn't dig himself out. He howled until Mother couldn't stand it and set him free. I leashed him to a post with a cow chain. He pulled himself away and ran off with the chain. When I heard him howling down by the river and went to investigate, I found his chain caught in a thick bush. He made the situation worse by running around the bush until he got himself so tangled he couldn't move. He was lucky the coyotes didn't get him."

"There must be something we can do to keep the two dogs apart."

"I don't know what it would be. I suppose we could shoot one of them."

With that kind of a response I decided to drop the matter, but a thought did cross my mind. If the running bosom buddies were reported to the game warden, they would both be shot.

We had finished eating and were still sitting around the kitchen table, drinking tea and talking, when Rusty came home. He barked to come in, and I opened the door—there he stood. His winter coat of thick red fur was completely covered with frozen snow. He recognized me immediately and his tail started wagging incessantly. He was happy to see me home again. I cupped my hand around his head and asked, "Rusty, are you still my dog?" He let out a long, mournful whine.

This scene happened many seasons ago; yet every year at Christmastime it comes back to haunt me. Did the little red dog sense what fate had in store for us? Was his long, mournful whine an omen of the quickly approaching day when he and I would be left alone to console each other? Sometimes I just ponder over it all; sometimes I cry.

Rusty came in from the bitter cold, blustery outdoors shivering, thirsty, and hungry. He ran for his water bowl and lapped up every drop of liquid. He gobbled up all his puppy chow and wanted more. I picked up all the skins from the Kentucky Fried Chicken we had for dinner and dropped them in his dish. He swallowed them up without even chewing.

I had to heat up a stack of terry towels in the oven to melt the snow clinging to the coat of red fur and to dry it off so it was fluffy again. He lay down on his favorite throw rug in the living room and was soon sound asleep.

Rusty hung around the house and followed me from room to room during the day. In the evenings, as soon as I sat down in my favorite chair, he jumped up on my lap and stretched himself across my knees with his head on the wide arm of the soft leather chair. I scratched his ears and stroked his fur coat, and he lay there, contented. At bedtime, he came up the stairs to my room and slept on the braided rug beside my bed When the alarm rang in Joey's room in the morning, Rusty stood up, placed his front paws on my bed, and woofed until I got up. We came down to breakfast together.

My original intentions were to stay with Mother and Joey until New Year's Day; but the weatherman's warning of an approaching snowstorm changed my plans and I was leaving three days earlier. Joey walked me to my car, and Rusty tagged along. He looked at me with his big brown eyes and a sadness in them I had seen before—in a little red dog at a puppy mill waiting for me to take him home.

As I drove away from the house, I saw Mother watching at the living room window. Rusty stood with Joey on the porch. Joey was waving his hand, but the little red dog was not wagging his tail.

Two weeks after returning to work, I received a long-distance call at school—a call that would drastically change the rest of my life. Joey was dead. He had suffered a heart attack. Mother was in the intensive-care unit of a hospital thirty miles away from home, where she died of bronchial pneumonia.

That night, for the first time in my life, I was alone in the old farmhouse. I decided to sleep in the downstairs bedroom. I threw an old quilt on the sofa in the living room and told Rusty, "You stay here!" But as soon as I pulled up the covers, he came into my room and jumped on the bed. I got up and carried him back to the sofa. "Now, you stay," I told him in a stern voice.

I tried to close the bedroom door, but the ninety-year-old door and the frame around it were both warped. The locking mechanism would not line up, and the door would not shut. I could not put the dog outside. It was a bitter cold night with high winds and temperatures hovering below zero.

Before I could settle back in bed, Rusty pushed the door open and was right back beside me. I was not happy sharing my bed with a dog, but I was too tired to get up and start moving furniture against the door. He put his head on my pillow and slept all night, cuddled up against my back.

Two days later, I walked behind two caskets and twelve pallbearers into the church for the funeral service. The burial would have to wait till spring.

A group of women prepared brunch at the farmhouse, and the friends and neighbors who attended the church services came to the house and spent the afternoon with me. Then all left and Rusty and I were alone.

We both retreated to the living room, where the crackling of birch logs in the fireplace felt comforting. I sat down in Mother's brown rocker near the fireplace. Rusty came and laid his head in my lap. I began to sob uncontrollably. He began to howl mournfully. And the wailing winds whistled around the corners of the old farmhouse, rattling the windows and shaking the doors. It was the end of a sad day; it was the end of a family.

I was given a week off from school to take care of my affairs. There was so much that had to be done before I returned to work. My biggest problem was Rusty. I called the apartment manager for permission to bring him back with me. She replied, "No way! If I permit you to keep a pet, then others will want to do the same. Soon we would have a dog, cat, or bird in every apartment."

One of Joey's friends wanted Rusty, but I could not bring myself to give him up. To me, at that time, it would have been the same as giving up my brother or mother. I needed someone to keep my dog for me until I returned to the farm for the summer. The neighbors were aware that I was considering retirement; however, they had some concerns: After living in a big city for over forty years, would I be happy living on the farm again? No one believed I would move back permanently. No one wanted to "get stuck with the dog."

Finally, John Nelson, my nearest neighbor, said to me, "Leave Rusty on a leash in the woodshed and I'll keep an eye on him and see that he has food and water," but the offer left me with little comfort. Although Rusty ran outside during the day, he returned to a warm house at night, where he had his own pad behind the wood stove in the kitchen. It was a cozy corner. The thought of him sleeping in the woodshed on cold winter nights was more than I could bear, but I had no other choices. I agreed to the plan.

Three times, during that long cold winter I had hoped to make a trip to the farm and called John. Each time, he told me, "Our roads are snow-covered and icy. Stay where you are and don't worry about Rusty. He's doing OK."

It was the first week in April before I ventured up north. When I arrived at the house, Rusty was on his leash. At first, he eyed me suspiciously. I released him. He went wild. He ran around me in circles and barked; then he leaped up in the air, almost to my shoulders, and tried to lick my face. I unlocked the front door, and he followed me into the house, where he ran from room to room, sniffing close to the floor, as if he was searching for someone.

During my two-day stay at the farm, Rusty ran freely. Only once did he run off with Smokey, but in a short while he was back, scratching on the door, wanting to come in. The day I left for the city, I put him on his leash. He didn't whine; he didn't wag his tail. He just stood there and stared at me. It was his way of telling me *Why are you doing this to me?*

At some time during the day after I left, Rusty pulled himself free and followed the car tracks to the main highway. Heavy traffic obscured their scent, and he became confused. As he wandered along the highway, farther and farther away from home, a driver spotted him. The driver stopped to pick up the dog and recognized him as the little red dog he had seen leashed at a farmhouse on one of the country roads.

The man picked up Rusty and took him home with him. He had lost his father recently, and just before the father died he told him, "If there is a reincarnation, I want to come back as a little red dog." So when the man brought home the little red dog, the whole family was elated.

In the meantime, John and all the neighbors were searching for my dog. Three weeks later, when John was coming home from work, he spotted Rusty on a leash at one of the houses along the highway. He pulled into the yard, and a woman came out of the house.

"You know whose dog this is?" John asked her.

"We know whose dog he was, but they're all dead. Aren't they?"

"No, they're not. One of them is still very much alive and she wants her dog back."

Reluctantly the woman unleashed Rusty, and John brought him back home. I was not told about the incident until after I retired and returned to the farm permanently. Then both John and the man who had picked up Rusty on the highway told me their versions of the incident.

I did not want to leave Detroit, and for five months I drove all over the metropolitan area searching for a condominium where I would be permitted to keep my dog. I found none. In the meantime, the rural post office was forwarding letters to me from realtors—all had buyers for the farm even though it was not listed for sale.

The morning that I was leaving to spend the summer up north, my friend Ellie stopped in to see me. I said, "Ellie, it looks as if I may have to return to the old farmhouse. I can't find a place that will let me bring Rusty."

Ellie was shocked. "Are you out of your mind?" she screamed at me. "How can you give up dancing at balls all over the city, eating at the finest of restaurants, attending

127

the many cultural activities, and give up your beautiful apartment to live in that vermin-infested home?'' She stopped for a moment to catch her breath; then added, "And all that for a little red mutt!''

The last time Ellie visited at the farm, mice in the attic above her room had kept her awake all night. Father had stored some prize corn in the attic to use for seed in the spring. The mice ran around the bushels of corn, having a ball. Ellie never forgot it.

I returned to the farm. During the long summer, Rusty and I walked the old gravel roads, tramped through the overgrown green fields and woods. We often stopped along the banks of Black River and watched the rainbow trout swim around the old wooden bridge. The world around me was permeated with tranquility, but my inner world was in a state of turmoil—filled with confusion, anxiety, mental anguish, and resentment. All the plans I had so carefully made for my retirement years were now hung out "on hold.''

The retirement gift I had planned for myself was a trip around the world. The tour originated in New York and returned to the States by way of San Francisco. On my return, a new career awaited me. After passing the examination for my license, I was offered a position with a real estate agency located in one of the elite suburbs of the city. The opportunity to show clients through the beautiful old mansions that were coming on the market was very exciting. The life that I had planned and the life that I was now living were worlds apart. The events of one week changed it all.

I sat on the porch with Rusty one afternoon, pondering about it all, when a real estate broker drove into the yard. I recognized him as one of the more persistent agents.

"It sure is a beautiful afternoon, isn't it?'' he greeted me, then went on, saying, "I had a young professional couple come to my office today. They are looking for a large farmhouse with some acreage. They are renting just a few miles north of here and like the area."

"Why would I want to sell the house, or any land, if there is a possibility I may be moving here permanently?"

"It's an old house and too big for just you and your dog. And what are you going to do with eighty acres? Why don't you build yourself a new house in the middle of that beautiful knoll on the east forty and sell the rest?"

A new house on the east forty? That possibility had not occurred to me. Suddenly I saw a light at the end of the dark tunnel. If I kept the east forty, I would also have the river and most of the forest.

The agent quickly noticed the glint in my eye, the expression of surprise on my face. "What do you think?" he asked.

"I don't know. I would have to find a builder first; even then, it is doubtful that the house would be completed before winter set in. I don't want to leave the dog alone another winter."

The agent left, but as he was getting into his car I heard him whistling. He was sure he had his foot in my door. Two hours later he called: "My clients would like to see the house. And if they buy it, they said they would take the dog, too."

Tom and Lori Brandon were a personable young couple. Rusty bonded with them immediately. He remained in the house where he had lived since he was three months old. I returned to the city, satisfied that I had made the right decision.

It was too late to take the trip around the world. The group had already sailed. My enthusiasm for the real estate business soon waned when I discovered that I would have to work evenings and weekends driving prospective buyers around the city. The social climate of the city was also changing—crime, of every kind, was increasing all over the town. The city that had been my home for over forty years was no longer appealing. I would have a house built on the east forty and move back to the farm.

Eight months later, I returned with all my possessions. The movers set up all the large pieces of furniture and left the boxes of small items in the garage for me to unpack. As I was sorting things out, I thought I heard scratching at the garage door. I opened the door and there was Rusty. I expected him to go wild with excitement, but he came in cautiously, sniffed at the boxes, and sniffed at me. Not until I asked, "Rusty, are you still my dog?" did he wag his tail. He followed me into the house and slept at the foot of my bed, just as he did when we stayed together in the old farmhouse. I let him out in the morning. He did not return.

That morning, my neighbor John dropped in to see me on his way to work. From him I learned that Rusty had bonded very well with the Brandons. They took him everywhere with them—on hikes through the woods and down country roads, swimming in Lake Huron on hot summer days, and on Sunday rides and for dinners with relatives. He slept on their living room sofa when in the house and ran around with Smokey when they were at work. He was a free spirit.

Rusty never again was totally my dog. Like a child of divorced parents, he divided his time between the Brandons and me. During the week, when they were working, he stayed with me, but on weekends he returned to the old farmhouse. He did, however, come back to spend the nights with me. He slept on my lap while I watched television, and when I got one of my crying spells he cried with me. When we went walking, I no longer had to keep him on a leash. He ran ahead of me, and if I lagged too far behind he stopped and waited until I caught up with him,. Although, I had him only part-time, I found his company comforting.

For two years I shared Rusty with the Brandons and with John's big black Lab, Smokey, but I didn't mind. The little red dog had enough love for all of us. Then one morning, a Saturday before Easter, I opened the front door and Rusty took off. I never saw him again.

When Rusty had not returned by late afternoon, I called the Brandons. He was not there, nor had they seen him that morning. I walked over to John's place to see if Rusty was there with Smokey. John was out in the yard. Smoky was sleeping on his rug on the front porch.

"John, is my dog running around here somewhere?"

"He was here this morning. He and Smokey took off down the road, but Smokey came back about an hour ago. Rusty was not with him."

I returned home, got in my car, and drove up and down the country roads, and swamps for hours but found no trace of a little red dog. We visited humane societies and contacted veterinarians and the local sheriff. We placed an ad in the local paper with Rusty's picture. There were no reports from anywhere. Rusty had just completely disappeared.

For a long, long time I waited for the day when I would open my front door and find a tired, hungry little dog waiting to come into my house. That day never came.

Oh, Joey, Can You Hear Me Cry?

Sitting in a cozy rocking chair by the fireplace in the old farmhouse, I am sipping coffee and listening to the crackling of birch logs as they burn in dancing flames of yellow and orange. From here I can look out on the winter landscape, through the large boxed window facing the north, and watch all the things a northwest wind can do. With howling mirth and racing speed it is blowing all the small white clouds toward Lake Huron. Under the sailing clouds, against a pale blue sky, the white birches sway from side to side, like dancers on New Year's Eve singing "Auld Lang Syne." But it is not the song of the trees I hear; it is the wailing and whistling of the wind playing tag with the naked branches of the swaying trees. Now and then, the wind's chilling cold fingers dip down toward the fields and pick up leaves and twigs among the dry grasses, papers, and milk cartons from trash piles, and hurl them all unmercifully into the fence. There they are deposited in the wire mesh and will remain, under the banks of snow, until spring. Around the bird feeder, not a bird has chirped or a squirrel shown its tail all day, and the deer have retreated deep into the woods and hidden in the evergreens. It is another cold January day in northern Michigan.

Three years ago, on a cold January day such as this, I walked alone behind two caskets and twelve pallbearers. A small group of friends and neighbors, who braved the hazardous icy roads and banks of drifting snow, followed in procession behind me as the church bells tolled mournfully. Mother and brother Joey were being buried on the same day. They were the last of my family. As the procession moved toward the church, my whole body shook uncontrollably—not only from the biting wind and bitter cold but even more from the stark realization that I now was all alone. I had survived my parents, two sisters, and two brothers. Each death brought its share of tears and, for a while, the terrible pain of a great personal loss; but time had a way of healing the pain and leaving only the memories of times and a family that would never be again. I learned when it was time "to let go." Why, oh, why, can I not do the same with Joey? Three years have gone by since that January day, yet I cannot listen to the wind nor watch the snowflakes fall without reliving it all again. Sometimes I wonder if Joey can hear me cry, and when the winds wail around the corners and through the broken eave pipes of the old gray house it seems as if they are crying for him, too.

I remember the day Joey was born. It was a Sunday in May and Memorial Day. At the time, we were living on the west side of Detroit. Our four-room flat was above a grocery store, which was a front for the Blind Pig. Dark, threatening clouds hovered over the city all morning, hiding the sun. The afternoon brought thunder, lightning, and rain showers. I did not go out to play all day. Shortly after supper, Mother complained she was not feeling well. Father went downstairs to call the doctor. My oldest sister, Leocadia, took me and the twins, Michael and Michaelena, to Aunt Josephine's house, which was only two blocks down the street. Later that night, we were told we had a baby brother and his name was Joseph.

A few weeks later there was a big christening party for our baby brother. Father had chosen two close friends for

Joey's godparents. Both came from the same village in Poland as Father. Both were bootleggers. There were many arguments between my parents before the christening day. Mother objected to having bootleggers for her son's godparents, but in our family Father made the decisions. The bootleggers became Joey's godparents. The godmother was beautiful—a slender woman with dark brown bobbed hair, warm brown eyes, and the complexion of a Dresden china doll. Her carriage was regal; her manner, elegant. The beautiful expensive dresses she wore were purchased from a fashionable downtown shop. The godfather was a jolly man who like to tell amusing stories. He was short and on the stout side. The pinstriped suits he wore were custom-made by one of the best tailors in town.

The festivities on christening day began early on a Sunday afternoon. The tables were laden with platters of breaded pork chops and Polish sausage, bowls of mashed potatoes with mushroom gravy, and sweet and sour cabbage. Crispy angel wings, sprinkled with powdered sugar, and fancy pastries were served with the tea and coffee. The godparents supplied a keg of moonshine for the celebration. After dinner, the moonshine flowed freely. With each progressive round of drinks the boisterous merriment got louder. It was well into the evening when the keg went dry and the revelers went home. So ended the day Joey became a Christian.

Joey never got to know his godparents. He was two years old when he left the city for the farm in northern Michigan. Joey's godfather died shortly after we moved. Joey's godmother came to the farm only one time, for his third birthday. Joey squealed and jumped with joy when she presented him with a shiny red wagon and a big straw hat. Several pictures were taken of Joey with his gifts. The godmother had one of the pictures enlarged and mailed it to us in a beautiful brown-and-gold frame. It showed a little boy with spindly legs wearing high-buttoned shoes and a navy blue romper suit. It did not show his brown eyes, the red hair almost the color of the maroon wagon; nor the frail body hidden under the fullness of the romper suit. By the time Prohibition ended, the beautiful, elegant godmother had become a hopeless drunk. She was forty years old when she died. Alcohol killed both of Joey's godparents.

I don't know when Joey started drinking. He was still in grade school when I left the farm. The first years I was away, I rarely saw him. Whenever I came home for the holidays or an occasional weekend, he was seldom home. His friends were always showing up at the house at suppertime, and Joey would take off with them, often before he finished his meal. The more vehemently Father protested, the faster Joey ran out of the house. Time and time again, he did not return home until after midnight.

One Saturday morning, when I was changing his bed, I saw that he had thrown up during the night. The sight was extremely disturbing. I had visions of him choking to death some night on his own vomit. His driver's license lay on the nightstand. It had been altered to make his age twenty-one. He was eighteen years old.

Joey was born with a great talent—music. He had a great tenor voice. Not only could Joey sing, but he also could play any instrument he picked up just by exploring with it for a while. During his freshman year in high school, the band instructor offered Joey any instrument he chose to play and private lessons after school, both free. Father would not permit Joey to stay after school. He saw no usefulness in music lessons; besides, he needed Joey at home in the evenings to help out with the farm chores.

After Joey graduated from high school, he drove a truck for a local building contractor. With this job came the habit of stopping at the local tavern after work for a drink with the guys. Two-Beer Joey, they called him in those days. He may have had two beers at the bar, but as soon as he walked into the house he headed for the refrigerator and the third bottle of beer, which he quickly finished off before supper.

The construction work was seasonal. In northern Michigan, houses were not built during the frigid winter months. There was a three- or four-month layoff period with nothing to do but draw unemployment compensation. Every Friday, Joey drove his blue Plymouth coupe the forty-mile round-trip to the town of Alpena for his check. After cashing the check, he always stopped at one of the taverns in town.

The road that Joey traveled every week had two treacherous curves. One dark winter evening as he came around one of those curves, he drove his coupe into the back of a slow-moving trailer. His car was a total wreck. Joey claimed the trailer had no taillights. The damage to the trailer was extensive. The doors had fallen off, the windows broken, the contents strewn over the highway—boxes of canned goods, cooking utensils, clothing, books, and a little gray stuffed poodle. Miraculously, no one was injured. The trailer was a homemade job. The owners, a young couple, were returning to college after a midterm break.

One of our neighbors was also in town that day. He was driving a short distance behind Joey's car when the accident occurred. From him we learned that Joey could not walk a straight line and reeked of alcohol, that all who stopped at the scene of the accident sympathized with the young couple and expressed anger at Joey. One even called him a drunken son of a bitch. The two state troopers who responded to the accident did not treat him too kindly, either. One grabbed him by the shoulders, shook him, and pushed him in the backseat of the police car. The troopers charged Joey with driving while under the influence of alcohol, and took away his driver's license.

At the farmhouse that evening, concern for Joey was growing. Where was he? What was keeping him? No matter how late he left home, he was always back by suppertime. About nine o'clock that evening, there was a loud knocking at the front door. Father opened the door. There stood Joey, escorted by two state troopers. Father led the three into the living room. One of the troopers explained to father what had happened. Without saying a word, Father walked up to Joey. Using his right hand, then the left, both with palms fully extended and with the full force of his two-hundred-pound frame behind them, he slapped Joey across the face. Joey left the room and staggered up the stairs to his room. While Father was still sputtering in anger about his good-for-nothing son, Mother took a plate of food up to Joey.

As the troopers were leaving, one of them turned to Father and said, "Violence is not going to solve the problem. The young man needs help."

The driver's license the troopers took away from Joey was a special license. He needed it to drive the truck on the construction job. When he consulted with a local attorney, Joey was informed that it would be possible to get the license back, but it would cost a lot of money. Money was something Joey did not have. His wages were minimal; the work, not steady. Friends, however, he did have. Among his many friends was a man who owned the county newspaper. He had, at one time, worked for the state liquor commission and had friends and connections in high places. Some owed him favors. Without costing Joey a penny, he not only got his license back, but also all charges against him were dropped.

When the United States first entered World War II, Joey was too young for military service. Later, when he could have been drafted, Father applied for an exemption, stating that he needed his son to help operate the farm. Then came the Korean War. There were no exemptions. Joey was ordered to report for induction and sent to Fort Leonard Wood, Missouri, for training. From there he was sent to Germany for a two-year tour of duty with the 581st Engineering Field Maintenance Company. How thankful we were that he was not sent to Korea.

Joey enjoyed his stay in Germany. He spent some time in France on special assignment and visited Switzerland on leave. When he got his discharge from the service, he stopped in Detroit and spent a week with me before returning to the farm. The two-year tour of duty had been good for him. He appeared to be more confident and not so nervous. He had put some weight on his five-foot-ten frame. I noticed that his appetite had improved and he was not drinking as much. When he did drink, he got a mischievous twinkle in his eyes. He had a rich masculine voice, and it was good to hear him laugh. We went shopping for new civilian clothes. One night we went to one of the big-city nightclubs for dinner and the show. Dressed up in his new dark brown suit, a gold shirt with beautiful cuff links, and a gold-striped tie I saw a very handsome young man. Joey was now twenty-seven years old.

The maintenance training in heavy-duty equipment Joey had received in the army helped him to get his first steady job, and the pay was good. The county road commission hired him to drive one of their big trucks. During the summers, he helped build and maintain the county roads; during the winters, he cleared the ice and snow. He enjoyed his work. He liked his supervisor and the men he worked with. Just as in the days when he was working with the construction crew, he stopped every day after work for a drink with the guys.

Father continued farming, but his health was failing. His joints were getting stiff with arthritis, and he was taking digitalis every day for his heart. Whether it was his failing health or his age, he had mellowed somewhat with the years. Only occasionally would he be his old tyrannical self. Joey, too, no longer was running to his room every time Father went into one of his tirades. He was able to stand up to "the old man." One Easter Sunday afternoon, when father stood at the front door and tried to keep Joey from leaving the house—he was objecting to Joey going to the tavern on such a holy day—Joey pushed him aside with, "Listen, old man; I am thirty years old. You aren't going to tell me what I can or cannot do."

Father shouted back, "I don't care if you're a hundred and thirty years old! As long as you live under my roof, you are going to do exactly as I say!"

Joey headed for the front door, slamming it behind him with such force, I thought it would come off its hinges. When he returned home that night, he smelled so badly of alcohol, Toby, our mean German shepherd, did not recognize him. The dog grabbed Joey by the pant leg and ripped it off the trousers before Joey could calm him down.

In the year of his seventy-eighth birthday, Father decided to retire in the fall. He did not plant any crops that spring. He did not mow the hay fields that summer. His plan was to keep the cattle until the end of September, when the pastures began to dry up, then sell the whole herd at the big cattle auction. Father had worked hard all his life and was looking forward to the day when he could take it easy.

At the time, I was living in Detroit and teaching in one of the large city high schools. After living in the city for over twenty-five years, I had acquired an appreciation for country living. Every June, as soon as school closed, I headed for the farm. By then, the twins and my oldest sister were all dead.

139

Michael had died in the big fire that burned down the barn, a fire he had started by playing with matches. His twin, Michaelena, spent four years in a sanitorium before she died of tuberculosis. Leocadia, the oldest, suffered a heart attack at thirty-six. She, too, had been ill with tuberculosis for several years. Now there was just Joey and me. With each summer, the bond between us grew stronger, and we became very good friends. When Joey went bar hopping on weekends, I went with him.

It was the Friday night before the Fourth of July. As soon as I did the supper dishes, Joey and I headed for the tavern on the lake. This was a meeting place for all the boys and girls who had left the farm for the big city and now came home for the long holiday weekends. The dance floor was large, the band lively. The place was crowded and noisy. We stayed until the bar closed. It was three o'clock in the morning when we walked into the house. Both of us were "dead to the world" when Father got up that morning, had his usual cup of coffee, and headed for the barn.

A short while later, Mother picked up the milk pails and went to help him with the morning milking. She found the cows running around outside the barn, bellowing. Father was sitting on the floor near the door, leaning back against the manger. His hat had fallen into the manger. The cane he used to prod the cattle into the barn lay by his side. Mother ran out of the barn screaming. Her screams jolted Joey and me out of our beds. As fast as our legs would carry us, we raced towards the barn in our nightclothes. Father was not breathing. I ran to the house to call the doctor. Joey stayed and tried to revive Father with pulmonary resuscitation; but nothing would ever bring Father back. Not one day of his retirement did he live to enjoy.

A few months after Father passed away, Joey bought a small Cessna airplane. He had been flying with a friend for some time and now was taking private lessons. Joey earned his license quickly and soon was flying solo. He loved to fly. Any day the weather was calm, he hurried home from work, had his supper, and off he went into the wild blue yonder. He never drank on days he planned to fly. Never before had I seen him so contented and happy.

After Joey started flying, he had to have a complete physical every year before his pilot's license could be renewed. For a while, all went well then his blood profile came back showing high blood sugar. He was grounded, put on a diet, and told to stop drinking. He had to report to the doctor again in three months.

Joey continued going to the bar, but all he drank was ginger ale. It was unbelievable, seeing him sitting at the bar sipping ginger ale when all around him others were boozing it up. It did not seem to bother him. He told me he never felt better. Every day, rather than stopping with the guys for a drink, he came home and worked in the garage. He sawed boards and pounded nails; he sanded and polished the wood; then stained the finished project—a long workbench with drawers to accommodate all his tools. The oak staining was beautiful, and the bench looked more like an expensive piece of furniture than a workbench and storage for tools.

When Joey returned to the doctor, the second set of tests showed the blood sugar was back to normal; however, he was to report for more testing in another three months. When the time came, Joey canceled the appointment. He never went back to the doctor again.

That August, while I was still at the farm, Joey took his vacation, and traveled around Michigan for two weeks. When he returned from the trip, he came in the house carrying his suitcase in one hand and a six-pack of beer in the other. I was stunned. "Joey, what's this with the beer?" I asked.

141

"Oh, don't worry, Maria," he answered. "I'm just going to finish this off. I won't be getting any more. Really, I can take it or leave it."

I retuned to work at the end of August and did not come back to the farm until the middle of October. It was a beautiful Saturday morning when I drove Joey to the airstrip to fly his plane. After Joey took off, I stayed a while and visited with Bill Weston.

Bill was the owner of the small airport and a good friend of Joey's. We talked about Joey and his flying. Bill told me that Joey was a very good pilot; however, in the course of our conversation he blurted out, "No one around here ever thought the community drunk would be able to get a pilot's license."

The community drunk? The remark, coming from Bill, who was supposed to be one of Joey's best friends, cut me deeply. I left immediately. The remark did not. It stayed with me and nagged at me and kept me depressed for a long time.

Joey was not your usual drunk. There wasn't an ounce of aggression or arrogance in him. He never got into arguments. No bartender ever had to throw Joey out because he became a nuisance. I never heard him curse, swear, or use vulgar language. He disapproved of those who did. He was a friendly man, yet there was a certain reserve about him. After he had a few drinks, his eyes twinkled and he became talkative. If he drank too much, he came home, sat down in his reclining chair, and went to sleep.

His supervisor told me Joey was a very dependable employee. He was on the job every day and on time. His truck had the lowest repair cost record of all the truck drivers year after year. He could spot a problem before it became serious and made many of the repairs himself. He never drank on the job. There were men who did.

Joey was a kind and sensitive man, generous of his time when anyone needed help. For many years he went out of his way to pick up a widow for church every Sunday. He shopped for groceries for an elderly couple who didn't have a car. He helped neighbors shingle their roofs and pour cement for driveways and basements. He never accepted money. A bottle of beer was payment enough.

One cold rainy night, when Joey and I were sitting in the neighborhood bar, a man came in with his ten-year-old son. Shortly the man took up with a woman and they left, leaving the boy in the bar. When some time passed and the father did not return, the bartender asked the boy to leave. The boy's home was several miles from the bar—too far for him to walk on a cold, rainy night. He stood outside the bar in the rain, waiting for his father to return. Most of the patrons in the bar that night knew the boy, but it was Joey who left the bar to drive the boy home. Some saw my brother as the community drunk; I saw him as a gentle man and a gentleman.

After Father died, Mother became Joey's responsibility. He was very good to her. One day, she said to me, "All the widows around here envy me because I have Joey." One by one of the widows' children put them in nursing homes. Joey said he would never put Mother "in one of those places" unless it became absolutely necessary.

At first, after Father died, Mother was glad that Joey was not married. As she got older, keeping house became too much of a chore for her and she complained, "How long am I going to have to take care of him? I with he would get himself a wife."

I, too, was hoping that Joey would marry and have a family of his own, a son or two to carry on our family name. He had dated when he was in high school and was going steady with a very nice girl before he went into the service.

143

She wanted to get married before he left for Germany. He refused. When he returned, she was married to another man. Women were interested in Joey, but he had no interest in women.

Whenever I was home, Joey always had a cocktail hour before supper. As we sipped our drinks, we talked about many things. We reminisced about the old times; we discussed current problems; we made plans for the future. We discussed politics, religion, and literature. I was surprised to hear that during the winter when Joey was not working he did a lot of reading. Not only had he read many of the great American and English novels but also the French authors Flaubert, Hugo, and Zola and the Russians Tolstoy and Dostoyevsky. Joey also had read the Bible all the way through—both the Old and New Testaments. He often quoted from Scriptures as the occasion arose.

When I returned to work that fall, I returned as a counselor in a large inner-city high school. Over three hundred and fifty students were assigned to me, whom I not only had to keep academic and attendance records for but also was expected to discipline when teachers sent them out of their classrooms. When the weekends came, I was too exhausted to drive the two-hundred-mile trip home. I didn't return to the farm until the middle of October. The principal gave me permission to leave early that Friday, and I was home by four o'clock.

Joey should have been at work, but to my surprise I found him sound asleep in the recliner. I noticed he had a cut on his nose and his face was bruised. Mother was sitting in her rocking chair. Waving her hands in disgust, she told me in a sarcastic voice, "He's drunk again."

I hugged Mother, gave her a kiss, and started upstairs with my luggage. There were fresh spots of blood all the way up the stairs. Before coming back down, I decided to check

Joey's room. Two ashtrays were filled with cigarette butts, and the odor was sickening. A large hole was burned out in the small rug in front of his bed and another in the varnished wooden floor. *My Lord, he's going to burn the house down one of these days,* I said to myself.

Both Mother and Joey liked Kentucky Fried Chicken, and I brought a box home for supper. When the table was set, I woke up Joey. He shuffled his feet as he walked into the kitchen and toward the cupboard where he kept his bottle of whiskey. He poured himself a shot and swallowed it all down in one gulp before coming to the table. He nibbled at a drumstick and drank a cup of coffee, then returned to the recliner. He didn't ask me about my new position, nor did he say, "Maria, it's good to have you home."

When Joey came down to breakfast the next morning, his bruised face was swollen and he appeared haggard. I greeted him with, "I'm sure glad you're finally down here. Mother's been driving me crazy asking every few minutes, 'Where's Joey?' I must have answered it a hundred times, already."

His response was, "Let's see what you're going to be like when you get to be ninety years old."

I scrambled some eggs and fried some bacon. Joey made the toast. The three of us sat down to breakfast. Mother ate hers quickly and left the table. Joey and I sat for some time, sipping coffee and discussing Mother's problems. Joey was concerned that the time was quickly approaching when Mother would have to be placed in a nursing home. I couldn't believe it. She seemed so alert when I arrived home the previous day. Joey told me that he was doing all the cooking and most of the household chores. Jennie Nowak, our next-door neighbor, and Edie Weston, Bill's wife, were giving him some help. They were taking turns in looking in on Mother during the day when Joey was at work.

That October Saturday was a beautiful Indian summer day. The fall colors were at their peak. The trees in the woodstand back of the house were arrayed in various shades of yellow, orange, and red. Joey and I went for a walk in the woods that morning. We walked along the stream where the fish had come in to spawn. There were steelhead, rainbow trout, and a couple of brookies. A doe and her twin fawns stood on the opposite side of the stream watching us.

Joey stopped. He stood for a while as if in serious reflection. There was a touch of sadness in his voice as he quoted, " 'Like a deer that longs for running streams, my soul longs for you, My God.' "

Returning to the house, Joey had difficulty climbing the steep hill between the stream and the field in back of the house. It seemed that his legs just did not want to carry him.

I returned to the city the next day. I would not be back until Thanksgiving.

When I came home the day before Thanksgiving, Joey's lunch box was on the kitchen table. A sandwich and a small jar of canned peaches were still in the box. He, however, was nowhere around. Shortly, his friend Bill came looking for him.

I told Bill, "He should be at work, but his lunch box is here."

Bill answered, "Joey didn't work today. He's been hitting the bottle pretty heavy this week."

Joey got up that morning, packed his lunch, then for some reason decided not to go to work. Bill said he was repairing Joey's car and wanted to know if he should order all new parts or try to find some used ones.

"What's wrong with his car?" I asked. I was given some very disturbing news.

"Two weeks ago at three o'clock in the morning, Joey ran his car into a heavy steel rail on the main road to Oscoda," Bill answered.

"Oscoda, that's twenty miles from home. What was he doing there that time of the morning?"

Bill told me that Joey was no longer drinking at the local tavern. He had blacked out one night and fallen off the bar stool. The bartenders there refused to serve him anymore. He now was going to bars where no one knew him. Joey had been charged with drunk driving and destruction of public property and given a large fine. The judge also ordered Joey to report to Alcoholics Anonymous or his special driver's license, which he needed for his work, would be revoked. I had tried to get Joey to go to Alcoholics Anonymous when I came home in October, but he told me, "I can lick it myself. I did it before and I can do it again."

Joey didn't come home that day until seven o'clock in the evening. "Oh, you're home," he said when I met him at the door. I hugged him. He reeked of alcohol. His face and hands were icy cold. He wore a lightweight jacket, no cap, no gloves, nor boots—just some old oxfords. It was far from adequate clothing on a cold, snowy day when the temperatures hovered near zero. Joey sat down to the kitchen table and a plate of beef stew I set before him. He ate some of the stew, scraped the rest off his plate into the dog's dish, and headed for the recliner. He soon was sound asleep.

Thanksgiving morning, Joey went to the hunting camp. He did not take his gun. He said that he just wanted to see who all was there and visit with the guys.

I prepared the turkey and got it in the oven. While it was cooking, I cleaned the living room. There were burn spots all around the recliner. The ashtrays were loaded with cigarette butts and emitted an awful odor, which permeated the whole room. When Joey returned, I chided him on the holes in the rug, the unemptied ashtrays, and his heavy smoking. He also had to listen to statistics from all the articles I had read on smoking.

147

His response, "So . . . you're gonna live longer than I."

When the turkey was cooked, the three of us sat down to the Thanksgiving feast. Mother really enjoyed the turkey and dressing, the fresh cranberry salad, and the pumpkin pie. I made mashed potatoes with giblet gravy for Joey. He didn't like dressing.

When I left that weekend to return to the city, Joey walked me to my car. His last words to me were, "Don't go buying me a lot of clothes for Christmas. I won't be needing them."

I did not ask, "Joey, why are you telling me this?' What he was trying to tell me that morning did not register with me until I was on the main highway, heading toward Detroit.

For several years now I had been buying most of Joey's clothes. I always did my Christmas shopping early and already had Joey's gift—a pair of dark brown trousers with a matching jacket and a brown and gold plaid shirt. Joey's gift to me was to bring out of the woods the prettiest evergreen he could find. When I arrived home for the holidays, the two of us could decorate the tree together.

When I left home that Thanksgiving weekend, my intention was to return in two weeks to check on Mother and Joey. Weekend storms prevented me from making the trip. It was late in the evening two days before Christmas when I arrived at the farm. Joey was home. The tree was set up in the living room—a beautiful tree, loaded with small pinecones and extending all the way to the ceiling. The boxes of ornaments had all been brought down from the attic. Joey even had a pot of coffee perking on the stove. The five hours of driving in heavy traffic had been exhausting. I retired to bed early that night.

I awoke just before two o'clock in the morning and came downstairs to go to the bathroom. As I entered the living room, I saw a light in the kitchen. There was Joey standing at the cupboard where he kept the whiskey. I watched as he uncapped the fifth of Royal Canadian and drank straight from the bottle. I tiptoed into the bathroom and very quietly closed the door behind me. When I came out, Joey had already gone upstairs. He had not been aware of my presence.

The next morning at breakfast, I told Joey that I had seen him drinking in the middle of the night. He was quiet for a few moments; he picked up his cup of coffee and tried to bring it up to his lips.

"Look at me, Maria. I am an alcoholic."

His hands were trembling and the coffee was spilling from the cup over the table. I burst into tears and ran from the table into the living room. He did not follow me. After I composed myself, I returned to the breakfast table. We talked for a long time. He seemed to want to stop drinking, but the disease had taken such a hold on him, he no longer could help himself. I told him he should stop having liquor in the house and stay away from bars. He agreed that was the thing to do.

After breakfast, I started decorating the tree. Joey sat in the recliner, reading his Bible. He looked so thin, so pale, so weary. His nose was swollen and an awful purple color, his stomach bloated. Whenever he got up from his chair, he couldn't even pick up his feet. He just shuffled along. It was heartbreaking, seeing him in that condition.

Christmas Eve, we went to church; Christmas Day, we watched some television and listened to Christmas records. Late in the afternoon, we had a big prime roast beef dinner.

The next day, the county weekly newspaper came in the mail. It carried an announcement of an Alcoholics Anonymous meeting that was to be held that evening in the township hall. I planned an early dinner so Joey and I could attend.

149

Joey refused to go, saying; "It doesn't matter anymore. I am not going to be around much longer anyway."

"Joey, don't talk like that," I said. "You yourself said you licked it once before and you could lick it again. Just don't keep liquor in the house and stop going to bars." It was easier said than done.

After I returned to the city, I kept in touch with Joey by calling him twice a week. I always asked, "How are things going and how is Mother?"

He would respond, "Don't worry; everything is OK. I've got everything under control." But everything was not OK and nothing was under control. From the day I left, the situation had been getting worse day by day.

Then came Monday, January 12, a day that would drastically change my life. I was walking down the hallway, on my way to the lunchroom when a clerk came running from the main office calling. "Miss Markowski, there's a call for you from up north. It's Jennie."

I picked up the phone, expecting to hear that Mother was seriously ill. "Maria, I hope you're sitting down. I have some very bad news." Jennie hesitated for a moment, then continued, "Joey was found dead this morning, and the ambulance is here now to take your Mother to Emergency at Alpena General."

I dashed out of the school building, drove to the apartment for some clothes, and headed for the expressway.

When I arrived at the farmhouse, Jennie and her husband were waiting for me. She told me all that had happened that morning. When Joey did not report for work, his supervisor tried to contact him by phone. After trying for some time and not getting any response, he radioed Jim, one of the county men plowing snow in the area, to stop at the house and check out the problem. When Jim arrived at the house, all was quiet. There were no tracks anywhere on the freshly fallen snow. Joey's car was still in the garage. A shivering little red dog was trying to get into the house.

Jim knocked, but no one came to the door. He found the door was not locked and walked into the kitchen. There was Joey, sitting in the rocking chair, slightly slumped to one side. His right arm dangled over the side of the chair, his hand almost touching the floor. Joey was not breathing and his body was cold.

Mother was sitting in her rocker in the living room. She tried to tell Jim something, but she was unable to speak. Jim was trying to locate the phone in the house when Jennie arrived to look in on Mother. Jennie called the ambulance and the coroner. Then she called me.

I had a quick cup of coffee, and John drove me the thirty miles to the hospital. Mother was in the intensive-care unit. She was in a coma. The head nurse told me that Mother had bronchial pneumonia. I talked to Mother and held her hand. She did not respond.

That night, for the first time in my life, I was alone in the old farmhouse. I decided to sleep in the downstairs bedroom. The bedroom had a large open closet that ran under the stairway to Joey's room. I couldn't fall asleep. The lighted dial on the Big Ben alarm clock showed it was past 2:00 A.M. and I was still tossing and turning. At 2:30, which was the usual time that Joey came home from the neighborhood tavern, I heard the click of the light switch at the foot of the stairs, then heavy footsteps struggling up the creaking stairs. *Drunk again,* I said to myself. Startled, I jumped up into a sitting position. It couldn't be. Those footsteps would never be heard again. I must have dozed off and it was just a bad dream. The next morning, as I was dressing, the hospital called. Mother had died during the night.

For two days people came to the funeral home—friends, neighbors, parishioners from our church, Joey's work crew, veterans from the American Legion post, members from the Knights of Columbus, and the Good Fellows, so many people I had never met before. Over and over again I heard, "I knew him well," and, "Everybody liked Joey." The many good things I heard about my brother helped to ease the pain, but I also heard some comments that were very disturbing.

Joey's boss told me that he had not seen Joey at work for the past three weeks. One of these weeks was when I was home for the holidays. All that week, Joey had packed his lunch and left for work every morning at seven-thirty and returned home shortly after five in the afternoon. It was a week of bitter cold and blowing snow. Where did he go and what did he do all that time?

The bartender at the local tavern told me that the night before Joey died, to everyone's surprise, he walked into the bar. He had not been there for several months. He sat down at his favorite stool at the bar and ordered ginger ale. In the past, it had been his habit to walk from table to table, chatting for a while with everyone he knew. This night, he didn't move from the stool and he didn't say anything—not even to the bartender. He finished his drink and walked to the entrance door. When he reached the door, he turned around and stood there for a while looking around the room; then he turned on his heel and went out the door, and no one there saw him alive again.

The funeral director told me that their call at the farmhouse that day was one of the most bizarre situations he had ever come upon. In the kitchen, near the living room door, sat a dead man slumped over in his chair. In the living room, only a few feet from the kitchen door, sat a little old lady swaying back and forth in her rocking chair—oblivious to all that was going on around her. When he entered the living room, she stopped rocking and motioned for him to come closer. She tried to tell him something, but she could not talk.

After the funeral, some of the neighbors came to the house and visited for a while; then all left and I was alone again—just my dog, Rusty, and I. I poured myself a cup of coffee and sat down in the soft chair near the fireplace. Someone had built a fire, and it felt very comforting. The room held many memories, and soon the tears began to fall. Rusty was sleeping on a small rug in front of the fireplace. He got up, came over to my chair, and put his head in my lap. Uncontrollable sobbing and mournful howling filled the room, breaking the stillness of dusk that had begun to settle on the old farmhouse.

Two scenes of Joey keep flashing back in my memory. In the one scene, I see a young man sitting in a brown leather chair, teasing kittens with a long pair of shoelaces and laughing at their antics. The kittens, one jet-black and the other pale gray, are running up and down his long legs, up on his shoulder, and all over the chair. Their mother, a jet-black stray that had shown up on our front porch one morning, sitting on Mother's lap, purring and watching her kittens. In the other scene, I am looking out the large picture window of the living room. I see Joey walking up the path from the garage to the front porch. His blue denim jacket is swung over one arm, and he's carrying his black lunch bucket in the other. A little red dog is running alongside him, wagging his bushy tail.

Fifty-two years had gone by since our family moved from the city of Detroit to the eighty-acre farm in northern Michigan. Joey was two years old at the time. What happened during those years that drove him to drink himself to death? Was it our domineering father? Or was it some gene he had inherited from an ancestor he had never met? If Mother were living, she would say it was the godparents Father had chosen for his son.

On the desk in Joey's room in the old farmhouse stands an artistically ornamented copper plaque with the inscription: WHEN MY SHIP COMES IN I'LL PROBABLY BE AT THE AIRPORT. His ship never did come in. One cold day in January, far from shore, it sank in the turbulent waters of alcoholism.

> In my distress I called out to the Lord;
> he heard my cry and set me free.
> —Psalms 113:5

There Comes a Day of Reckoning

The long, shrill blast from the factory whistle brought the clanging noises of the production line to an abrupt halt, signaling the end of the workday for Charlie and his buddies at the Dodge plant on Detroit's east side. Also, it was Friday and payday.

It was customary for the group of men to meet at Big John's Saloon after work on Fridays. The saloon, located two blocks down the street from the main entrance of the plant, was across the street from the bus stop where most of the men boarded buses for the ride home. Big John's was a pleasant place for the men to gather, relax over drinks, and share in some camaraderie.

"Charlie, you joining us for a drink today?" one of the men asked as they were leaving the building.

"I am not sure, Tony. I have to make a stop at the butcher shop first. If I don't have to wait long to get waited on, I'll drop in for a short one. Save me a place at your table, just in case I do."

"Ok, Charlie, we'll be looking for you. Hope the line's not long."

When Charlie entered the butcher shop, the line not only was long; it was also at a standstill. A customer buying a chicken was the problem. The butcher was showing the woman one chicken after another, but he couldn't come up with one that pleased her. One was too fat, another too small, etc. etc. Finally, he reached down into the bottom of the stacked chickens in the meat case and pulled one out he hoped would meet with her approval; instead, the woman took a quick look at the bird and said, "It's got peculiar-looking legs."

The butcher's patience ran out, and he shouted at his customer. "Lady, are you buying a chicken to cook or to dance with?"

The waiting patrons roared with laughter, and the woman walked out in indignation without buying anything.

As the line began to move, Charlie pulled out of his hip pocket the slip of paper his wife, Nicole, had handed him that morning. To his surprise, all she had written was: "Two pounds of hamburger." A feeling of great resentment came over him. He felt his wife could have bought the meat herself at the large supermarket within walking distance of their home. He had some suspicions in the past, but now he was convinced that the only reason Nickie had him stopping at the butcher shop on Fridays was to deliberately keep him from joining his buddies for a drink at Big John's Saloon. The more Charlie thought about it, the more his resentment grew until it gnawed at him like an ulcer.

After Charlie left the butcher shop, he stopped at the bank to cash his check, then headed for the saloon His buddies were on their second round of drinks. He sat down in the chair they had saved for him and placed his small white package under the table. The waitress was busy and Charlie decided to go up to the bar and get his own drink.

"Your usual Molson Canadian?" the bartender asked.

"No, I think I will have a double scotch on the rocks instead of the beer."

The bartender was surprised. Charlie wasn't much of a drinker. Usually he would have just the one bottle of beer during his entire stay. Once in a while, when he came in late, he would have a shot of whiskey with water. Charlie picked up his drink and joined his buddies at their table.

"What took you so long, Charlie?" one of the men asked.

"Oh, some bitchy dame couldn't make up her mind what she wanted. The butcher must have shown her every chicken in the case and then she walked out without buying one."

"How come you have to shop every Friday? Your wife's not working, is she?"

"No, but she is very busy. She watches talk shows in the mornings and soap operas in the afternoon. The rest of the time she spends thinking up all sorts of chores to keep me occupied on weekends, especially if I have plans to go fishing or golfing. When she runs out of ideas, then her mother comes up with something for me to do. Last Saturday, I drove clear across town to my mother-in-law's house to fix a cupboard door she complained wouldn't close properly. When I got there, I looked the situation over, relocated a jar of sauerkraut and two sardine cans, and the door closed perfectly. Made me madder than hell."

"Must be difficult having to put up with two such demanding women," his buddy Tony responded sympathetically.

" 'Difficult' is putting it mildly. Before I married, I didn't go to church and I didn't believe there was a hell. It didn't take long for Nickie and her mother to straighten me out. I now attend church every Sunday and I know there is a hell—it's my marriage."

"How did you come to marry Nickie?" Tony asked.

"I have been asking myself that question ever since my wedding day, ten years ago. It all started at a singles dance at the YMCA one Saturday night. I was standing in the stag line, looking the place over, when this good-looking blonde with a come-hither smile walked up to me. She had sparkling brown eyes and full red lips, which matched the tangerine-colored chiffon dress she wore. The gal was easy to look at, and I asked her to dance. She was a great dancer—had great-looking legs, too, with very slim ankles. We danced together all evening and I asked her for a date."

Just then, the telephone rang and the bartender called out, "Charlie, your wife wants to know when you're coming home with the hamburger!"

"Damn her! Tell her I am already on my way and bring me another double scotch on the rocks."

The bartender was concerned about Charlie. He had never seen him in such a bad mood. Usually the tall, slender man was very quiet and presented a relaxed, casual appearance. The bartender filled a glass with cracked ice, poured only one shot of scotch in it, and carried it over to the table. As he placed the drink in front of Charlie, he said, "Drinking kinda heavy today, aren't you, Charlie?"

"I have my reasons," Charlie answered. He took a sip of the scotch and asked, "Where was I?"

"You were telling us how you happened to marry Nickie," Tony answered.

"I had dated her for three months when one Saturday morning I found myself standing in a reception line outside a church. Everyone was kissing Nickie and congratulating me. I stood there asking myself, *when did I propose?* To this very day, I can't remember ever proposing to Nickie."

All conversations ceased when a little old lady entered the bar through the side door. She looked like a bag woman, but she carried no bag with her. Her dark brown dress was terribly wrinkled and soiled. Her once-white ankle-high tennis shoes were badly in need of laundering. Her gray-streaked black hair hung down to her shoulders and needed a good combing. She was a pitiful sight. The woman walked from table to table asking, "Have you seen my husband?"

The patrons just shook their heads, indicating that they had not seen her husband. No one asked her any questions. The woman then went up to the bar and asked the bartender, "Have you seen my husband?"

"What's your husband's name?" the bartender asked.

"Joe Wilson," she answered.

"How long has it been since you saw Joe?"

Without hesitating, the woman answered, "Twenty years."

"My dear lady, if you haven't seen your husband for twenty years, it's best you go home and forget about him."

Jack had been working at the bar for five years. He had never seen the woman before and was curious as to where she came from.

"Mrs. Wilson, where do you live?" he asked.

The woman did not answer. She walked back to the side door and left. Jack picked up the phone and alerted the police to her presence in the area.

For the first time since Charlie entered the saloon, he laughed. "Smart guy, that Joe. Must have had a wife like mine. Walked out on her one day and never looked back—just kept on a-walking. Maybe that's what I should do."

Charlie finished his drink, and as he got up to leave Tony said to him, "Try to have a good weekend."

"Oh, I will, Tony. You can bet on it." He waved his hand and called out, "See you all Monday," as he went out the door to catch his bus.

The scotch Charlie had consumed in the short time was beginning to have an effect on him. The resentment and anger smoldering within him added to its potency, as did the length of time since he had his lunch of a bologna sandwich, doughnut, and coffee. Charlie had a hard time trying to climb the high step into the bus. Having to hold onto a package of meat added to the problem.

The bus driver left his seat and grabbed Charlie by his free arm. At the same time, the two men standing behind him on the outside lifted him into the bus. One of the passengers in the front seat got up and offered Charlie his seat, saying, "You can sit here. I am getting off at the next stop."

"Buddy, where you getting off?" the driver asked before he pulled away from the curb.

"Elm Street," Charlie answered.

With passengers getting on and off at every stop along the route, it took the bus an hour to reach Elm Street. Getting off the bus, Charlie stumbled on the high steps and dropped his package. The tape that held down the two folded edges snapped, and the paper began to unfold. He picked up the package with both hands and held it in front of him as he headed for the steps of the corner drugstore. He sat down in the middle step and placed the package alongside him. He placed his elbows on his knees and cupped his hands under his chin—and he just sat there.

A gust of wind flipped open the white paper wrapped around the meat and exposed the hamburger. In a few minutes two black cocker spaniel puppies came running down the driveway between the drugstore and the neighboring house. They headed straight for the hamburger and quickly gobbled up all the meat. They then circled around Charlie several times, sniffing for more of the good stuff. When they were convinced that he did not have any more, one of them picked up the empty meat wrapper in his jaws and headed back home. The other puppy followed.

Charlie knew if he went home without the hamburger there would be hell to pay. He stayed on the steps and pondered about an alternative. Several options kept popping up in his head. He decided not to go home; instead, he would hop a bus going downtown and stop at Carl's Chop House for one of their prized blue-ribbon Black Angus beef dinners. As Charlie started across the street for the bus stop, he noticed a taxicab pulling away from the curb a short distance down the street. It was coming his way, and he flagged it down.

"Carl's Chop House," he told the driver as he entered the taxicab.

The Chop House was situated near the Olympia Stadium, home base of the Detroit Red Wings hockey team. It was rated among the finest of the city's restaurants for its excellent food and elegant atmosphere. Hockey fans filled it to capacity on game nights.

"You must be going to the hockey game," the cabbie commented.

"I forgot there was a game tonight," Charlie answered.

"You may have to wait a long time to be served. Want me to take you somewhere else?"

"No, I am wondering if I can still get a ticket to the game."

"The general seating may be all sold out, but if you want just one ticket, you might still be able to get one of the more expensive seats."

"Drive me to the box office. If the line is not long, wait for me."

The general seating was all sold out, and no one was waiting at the ticket window. Charlie bought himself a choice ticket.

"Got one," he showed the cabbie as he reentered the taxicab. "Hope I am that lucky at the restaurant."

When Charlie entered the restaurant, a pretty young brunette greeted him at the door with a cheerful smile. "How many in your party?" she asked.

"I am alone," he answered.

The hostess escorted him to a small table in a corner, near the kitchen. It was set up for two and used only on days when the restaurant was filled to capacity. Very shortly, a waitress brought him the menu and asked, "Would you care to order a drink?" He ordered a glass of claret.

Charlie studied the menu and when the waitress returned with the wine, he was ready to order. He chose the herring in sour cream for the appetizer, a tossed salad with blue cheese dressing, a baked potato, and a porterhouse steak, medium rare. The service was efficient; the food, delicious. Charlie cut into the juicy, tender steak, savoring every morsel and telling himself, *Sure beats eating hamburger.* He was grateful to the cocker spaniels who had saved him from another monotonous Friday night supper.

The wine and festive atmosphere helped Charlie relax. Not having Nickie at the table, telling him all about the odd jobs she had planned for him to do over the weekend, was another bonus. He felt good about himself and had no regrets for the decision he had made—one he had thought about for some time but never had the courage to carry out. Changes needed to be made in his marriage. He had taken the first step.

Charlie walked the short distance from the restaurant to the stadium. On his way, he spotted the large sign atop the YMCA building between the stadium and the downtown area. He often drove by the tall red building and knew their rooms were available for rent to the public. It would be a good place for him to stay overnight and think about tomorrow.

The thought of tomorrow released a twinge of conscience in Charlie. It kept telling him, *You must call Nickie and let her know you won't be coming home tonight.* He would call her during the game's intermission. The outcome of their conversation would determine if and when he would return home.

Charlie's choice seat offered him an excellent view of the ice rink and the fast-moving, exciting game. The Red Wings were in the winning for the National League Championship, and this night they were playing their chief contender—the Toronto Maple Leafs. Every time the Wings scored a goal, the fans went wild. Charlie was enjoying himself immensely. He realized how much he had given up in his ten-year marriage to Nickie. Not once in the ten years had he attended a Red Wings game. Seldom did he get to see the games at the Detroit Tigers' stadium. He gave up his Saturday morning workouts at the Community Recreation Center and bowling with his shop buddies in the league games on Wednesday nights. Any time he wanted to go off "on his own" for a while, Nickie made a fuss. It was so exasperating.

Of all the activities Charlie gave up, he resented most of all the frequent trips he made to visit his parents and two sisters on their farms in northern Michigan. Nickie never wanted to go—she said she didn't like farms, but he knew what she really meant was that she didn't like his family. They didn't care for her, either. Charlie was thirty years old at the time of his marriage, and Nickie was twenty. His parents found their daughter-in-law very immature. They felt that their son would have done better had he married a woman closer to his own age.

Just before intermission, Charlie headed for the phone booth in the lobby. He carried all his grievances with him. He dialed his home number, and Nickie answered on the first ring. She had been sitting by the phone, waiting for the call.

"My Lord, Charlie! Where are you? I've been worried sick that you might have met up with some kind of accident.

163

I called the bar; I called Tony. I even called the police. The only information I was able to get was the time you left the bar."

"Worried sick about me, are you? Well, you needn't be. I am at the Olympia, watching the Red Wings play Toronto and having a great time. Had a great dinner, too, a porterhouse steak at Carl's Chop House."

"Charlie, are you drunk?"

"No, I am not."

"What's gotten into you?"

"Nothing's gotten into me. I've just come to my senses."

"What does that mean?"

"It means that from now on, I am taking charge of my own life—no more errand boy; no more handyman. I am not coming home tonight," he answered.

The quiet voice became loud again as Nickie screamed out at her husband, "You are not coming home tonight? Just where is it you're planning to stay? You haven't picked up with some woman, have you?"

"The thought never occurred to me, but it's something to think about."

At that point Nickie hung up and Charlie returned to the game. He was relieved to have gotten the dreaded conversation over with; he began to relax again. Eventually, he would have to return home. Even if he didn't plan to stay, he still had to pick up his clothes and the new red Oldsmobile convertible coupe. The red color and the convertible top were not his choices—it was just the result of one of their many arguments that ended up in Nickie getting her way.

He wondered what kind of reception he would get when he did return. In the early days of their marriage, Nickie had always greeted him at the door, "Hi, handsome." He still was a very handsome man. His black hair was slightly streaked with gray, but it did not take away from his good looks; instead, it gave him an air of distinction. Perhaps, if he stayed away long enough, Nickie would realize how nice it would be to have Charlie around the house again.

The Allotment

On a beautiful wooded knoll facing the cold green waters of Lake Huron stands Mount Joy Cemetery, enclosed by a high gray steel fence and towering white pines. It is the oldest cemetery in the county and attracts both history buffs and genealogists.

May, with Memorial Day weekend, brings out many visitors. Some walk among the gray tombstones looking for a piece of history; others search for a familiar name of an ancestor who was known to have resided in the area. All are attracted to the red granite tombstone with the two large clumps of bleeding hearts. The plants, in full bloom, stand like sentinels, one on each side of the tombstone. The visitors stop to read the inscriptions:

James Clifford Cooper   Rosalyn Marie Cooper
Feb. 7, 1922–Mar. 28, 1946   June 18, 1922–Mar. 28, 1946

No "dear husband and wife"; no "loving father and mother"—just names and dates.

The curious, who notice that two people died on the same day, seek out some "local" who can answer their question, "What happened on March 28, 1946?" They will hear a tragic story, one that has been told time and time again. Some will hear it with a little added; some will hear it with a little omitted. Few hear it as it was.

Jimmie and Rosie lived on adjoining farms and were inseparable playmates in their early elementary years. She was a tomboy who went along with anything he wanted to do. They slid down the ropes from haylofts and climbed trees, searching for baby squirrels and birds in hollow tree trunks. When heavy rains flooded the Black River, which ran through both farms, Jimmie brought out his raft and Rosie helped him paddle it down the stream. They watched brookies and rainbow trout swimming under the old wooden bridge and tried to catch them. When winter came, they raced their sleds down the snow-covered hills and built snowmen. One day, Jimmie told Rosie, "When we grow up, I'm going to marry you."

As they grew older, Rosie preferred being with girls her own age, just talking and giggling. Jimmie shot marbles and played ball with the boys. Around her twelfth birthday, Rosie began to show a great interest in older boys. To Jimmie, she remained his favorite girl, the one someday he would marry.

During the high school years, the chubby little Rosie developed into a slender teenager, a brown-eyed blond, sensuous and sophisticated beyond her years.

Jimmie continued to hang out with the farm boys and girls, but Rosie was able to break into the elite group of city students to which Louis Martel belonged. The tall, dark, handsome young man had the physique of a Greek god. The only, and pampered, son of the wealthiest man in the county, Louis always had money in his pocket, wore expensive suits, and drove a "collegiate special" Plymouth sports roadster. Girls went wild over the dashing Louis and his burgundy car with the bright yellow wheels.

In their senior year, Louis was chosen president of his class and Rosie was voted the prettiest girl in the Mason County High School. They started dating. It hurt Jimmie deeply to see the pair, holding hands and kissing whenever they were together. Not once since entering high school had Jimmie been able to get a date with Rosie. Time and again he had asked her to go with him to the Saturday night dance at the Grange Hall, but she always had some excuse why she couldn't go.

Jimmie was a quiet, ordinary-looking farmboy. He did not get a regular allowance, owned no fancy suit, and drove his parents' old black Ford, which had been purchased at a used car lot. Rosie lost all interest in her childhood friend.

The summer after graduation, Jimmie helped his father out on the farm. He was extremely restless and very unhappy. He did not attend any of the Grange dances. He preferred staying home with a book or listening to the radio. There were girls who would have liked to date him, but he just could not get Rosie out of his mind.

In January of 1941, Jimmie enlisted in the Marines and immediately left for the Corps's recruit training depot at Parris Island, South Carolina. Very quickly he became a marksman skilled in the use of the rifle—an expertise that placed him in the First Rifle Regiment of the Marines' First Division.

When Jimmie returned home on his first furlough, he decided to drop in at the Grange Hall, just to see who was there. Wearing his blue dress uniform with the red and gold trim and white hat, belt, and gloves, he made an impressive entrance.

Rosie spotted him coming into the hall. She ran up to him and threw both arms around him, kissing him and gushing over him, "Oh, Jimmie, it's so good to see you. How handsome you look!"

Jimmie was still stunned when Rosie walked him out on the dance floor and they started jitterbugging to the beat of "Chattanooga Choo Choo." He wondered where Louis Martel was but did not ask. And Rosie did not tell him that she and Louis had a "falling out" and were not seeing each other.

The next morning at breakfast, Nellie Cooper asked her son, "Who all did you get to see last night?"

"I ran into Rosie and we danced the whole time together," he beamed.

"She wasn't there with Louis?"

"No, I didn't see him there."

"Then it must be true that he dropped her. You aren't planning on seeing her again, are you?"

"Yes, I am. We're going to the movies this afternoon to see Abbott and Costello in *Buck Privates*."

"Oh, Jimmie, I wish you weren't. People are saying she is even worse than her two sisters, and they both had to get married. Sarah had her baby only four months after the wedding. John Hanson had no intention of marrying Sarah until Archie Jenson told him he would shoot him dead if he did not marry her. John had already made plans to go to college, and he had to give that up and find a job to support Sarah and the baby. That Sarah ruined Johnny's whole life. He now spends more time at Charlie's Place, getting drunk, than at home with Sarah and the baby."

Nellie could have gone on and on, but Jimmie stopped her with, "Mother, I don't want to hear any more."

As Jimmie was leaving home that afternoon, Nellie warned her son, "Don't you let her talk you into getting into the backseat. You will be sorry."

Jimmie did not answer his mother. He left the house and slammed the door behind him.

Nellie Cooper was very upset. Her son was home for such a short time, and he preferred to spend his time with a girl who had a reputation as "being easy" and was referred to by some as "Louie's slut." Nellie prayed that her son's Christian upbringing would save him from the arms of a lustful woman. She told her husband, "Joe, you gotta talk some sense into that boy!"

When the time came and father and son were alone, Joe found it difficult to discuss women and sex with Jimmie. The conversation quickly turned to farm crops and cattle prices.

Rosie worked as a waitress in the dining room of a popular summer resort. They were very busy that summer, and she worked long shifts. She and Jimmie were not able to spend as much time together as they would have liked. But on her day off the last week of his furlough, they spent the whole afternoon at Charlie's Place, a local bar, listening and dancing to jukebox music.

At times, Jimmie found Rosie's behavior disturbing. When they danced, she draped her arms around his shoulders so tightly he had difficulty leading her around the dance floor. She played footsie with him under the table, and on one occasion he held hands with her just to keep her from massaging his "privates." Her kisses were becoming more and more passionate. He felt she was trying to seduce him, and it was making him uncomfortable. He had never had sex.

On their last time together, Rosie wanted to go up to the hayloft where they used to slide down the rope when they were children. He knew what would happen and refused. It wasn't that he did not want to make love to her. But every time he thought about it, visions of her making out with Louis Martel popped before his eyes. It turned him off. He left for camp still a virgin man. During the long and lonesome ride back to Parris Island, Jimmie slept on and off. Whenever he awakened, his thoughts returned to Rosie and he was sorry he had not made love to her.

A few days after his return to camp, Jimmie was surprised to receive a letter from Rosie. She wrote how much she had enjoyed the time they spent together and was looking forward to his next furlough. The letter ended with: "All my love, Rosie." He answered that same day, but it would be some time before he would hear from her again.

Shortly after Jimmie left, Rosie and Louis made up and were going steady again. She became pregnant. When she told Louis that she was carrying his baby and they would have to get married, he became very angry.

"No way!" he shouted at her. "How do I know it's mine?"

"It's yours all right and you are going to have to support it."

"No, Rosie, I don't have to marry you and I don't have to support your bastard. You will have to find some sucker to do that. Why don't you marry Jimmie? Then you can get an allotment. If he doesn't come back, you'll also get ten thousand dollars."

Rosie's ears caught every word Louis flung at her during their argument that evening, as she lay awake in the night she pondered them all. But in the morning, what dwelt most on her mind was "allotment" and "ten thousand dollars." She had a plan, but first she had to know when Jimmie would be coming home again.

Jimmie began receiving letters from Rosie twice a week. Her first letters were casual, containing news about people they both knew and events in the community. She wrote how much she missed him, how she was waiting for him to come home.

When Jimmie wrote back that he expected to be home for Thanksgiving and ended his letter: "Love you, my dearest, with all my heart. Counting the days when I can see your beautiful face again," she knew it would all be easier than she had expected. All her ensuing letters brought up marriage, and finally Jimmie agreed that they should get married when he came home in November.

171

When Nellie Cooper opened her son's letter and read that he would be coming home for Thanksgiving, she was elated. But as she continued reading the smile left her face and hot tears rolled down her cheeks. Never, never, would she accept Rosie Jenson for a daughter-in-law. Nellie sat down in her rocking chair and went into a fit of uncontrollable weeping.

Joe Cooper was in the woodshed, stacking wood, when he heard his wife's loud crying. He ran into the house and was frightened when he saw her in such a hysterical state. He called their daughter, Janet, who lived a few miles dow the road from her parents. The daughter and her husband, Jake, came over immediately.

Janet picked up the letter on the small table next to her mother's chair, read it and put it down, and she, too, wanted to weep. Janet contacted her brother at Parris Island, and both she and Jake tried to talk Jimmie out of the marriage. But it was all to no avail. Jimmie's mind was made up and no one was going to change it.

Jimmie came home and he and Rosie were married the day after Thanksgiving in the Community Baptist Church, to which his family belonged. He wore his blue Marine uniform. Rosie looked stunning in her floor-length off-white satin gown with the high neck bodice of Alęcon lace. A small beaded crown sat atop her fingertip veil. Rosie's mother was a dressmaker who had outfitted many a bride in Mason County. This time, she "really done herself proud." The young country boy and girl made a handsome couple.

After a reception in the basement of the church, where the Ladies' Aid put on their famous chicken dinner, the newlyweds left for their honeymoon at a small cabin Rosie had rented at the resort where she worked.

On her wedding day, Rosie was already two months pregnant, but no one knew. When she first suspected that she may be pregnant, she visited a doctor outside Mason County. She never told her mother or her two sisters about her condition. Only one person knew of her pregnancy, Louis Martel, and he was not about to tell.

The honeymoon was short, the furlough coming to an end. Jimmie had to return to Parris Island. As he sat on the train, waiting to pull out of Mason, he watched his family standing on the station platform, waving at him and crying. Rosie stood dry-eyed, preoccupied with her own thoughts. As the train pulled away, little did any of them dream that more than four years would pass before they would see one another again. For Jimmie, they would be four horrific years.

The train was still speeding toward Parris Island when the passengers were informed that Pearl Harbor had been bombed by the Japanese. A stunned silence fell over the passengers. Jimmie wondered what awaited him when he reached the base.

The First Marine Division, to which Jimmie belonged, was split into two groups. One group would sail from Norfolk, Virginia; the other, at a later date, from San Francisco. He was assigned to the San Francisco group. He would be leaving for New River, North Carolina.

Marines from all over came pouring into New River. Some were professional soldiers, the old breed of American leathernecks. Then there were the volunteers, high-spirited young men in their teens and twenties, fresh from boot training. They knew nothing about real war. They knew only what they had learned in boot camp. The Marines lived in pup tents, slept on the ground, and underwent more training as they waited.

The First Division left New River by train for San Francisco. When they disembarked from the trains, the ships were already waiting to take them out to sea and the war in the South Pacific.

Jimmie stood at the bow of the ship, looking out at the wide expanse of blue water and the fleet anchored in the San Francisco harbor. Marines crowded all around him, and yet he felt so alone. His thoughts turned to home.

He relived his honeymoon with the beautiful Rosie. He worried about his father, who looked so tired and was constantly complaining about his aching joints. Jimmie was hurt by his mother's animosity toward Rosie. He was happy for his sister, who had a wonderful husband and two handsome boys, and hoped that he, too, would have children of his own some day. He remembered the wonderful times he and Rosie had playing together when they were children. How different his life might have been if he could have married Rosie right after high school and not enlisted in the Marines. And he wondered if he would ever see her and his family again.

Jimmie's destination was New Zealand, a country in the South Pacific, one of the members of the British Commonwealth. But the time was quickly approaching when the sheltered, naive farm boy, who had never been away from home until he enlisted in the Marines, would be exposed to the most unbelievable horrors of death, destruction, and unimaginable carnage. He would suffer incredible hardships, extreme physical pain, and mental anguish.

Rosie's baby was born in June, seven months after her wedding. All three of Mary Jenson's first grandchildren came early, and she was telling friends and neighbors, "Premature babies run in our family."

When she told that to Dr. Miller, who delivered the babies, he replied in his usual gruff manner, "Mary, your grandchildren were all full-term babies. What runs in your family is a lack of sexual self-control."

Dr. Miller's nurse was Nellie Cooper's sister She told Nellie what she had heard. The two women kept the secret between them. They worried that should Jimmie find out that the baby was not his, he might deliberately get himself killed.

Rosie did not write to Jimmie that they had a baby boy until August, nine months after their wedding. She did not mention when the baby was born nor that she had named the boy Louis.

It would be a long time before the letter reached Jimmie. He was in Guadalcanal, fighting swarming hordes of vicious, fanatical enemy in the most hostile terrain in the world, a terrain of dripping rain forests and blistering sun, of flesh slashing coral and barbed wire, a malarial wilderness of dense jungles and poisonous swamps filled with burrowing, blood-sucking insects. Finally, Guadalcanal was taken by the Marines, but the First Division would fight again in the New Britain and Peleliu Islands.

On August 15, 1945, the war in the Pacific came to an end. Jimmie would be going home. He would be taking with him horrific memories he could never forget.

He had walked among the carnage of men torn to pieces by shrapnel and men still alive with their arms and legs severed from their bodies, blackflies feeding on their blood. He had heard the cries of the wounded and the screams of men so fatigued from combat they were going out of their minds. He had waded in waist-high water red with Marine blood. His own body knew the burning fires of malaria, the pain of flesh torn by jagged coral and skin cracked by the parching sun. He had suffered the gnawing pains of hunger and the discomforts of dysentery. He endured and he survived. Sometimes he wondered why.

On those rare nights when the monstrous bursts of gunfire from machine guns and exploding shells ceased and he fell asleep in some mud-filled foxhole, he dreamed he was home, holding Rosie and the baby in his arms. Perhaps it was these dreams that sustained his spirits and kept his emaciated body alive. Finally the living hell was over and he was on his way home.

As the train pulled into Mason, Jimmie watched anxiously for a glimpse of Rosie and their little boy. He saw several groups of people scattered along the platform, but his wife and son were not among them. He was the first to disembark, right into the arms of his waiting mother. She hugged and kissed him, and they both cried until the tears on their faces rolled together.

Nellie slipped her hands down her son's arms and stepped back to take a closer look at him. What she saw frightened her. He was so thin; he looked so exhausted. His face was a peculiar shade of gray, and his blue eyes were downcast. He was only twenty-four years old, yet when she watched him coming down the steps of the train toward her he moved like an old man. Her heart bled for him not only for all he had suffered in the past but also for what was yet to come.

When his mother released her hold on him, Jimmie's eyes searched the area for the two loved ones he so desperately longed to see—Rosie and the son he had never met. He could not understand why they were not there to meet him. An uneasy feeling came over him, and he could not bring himself to ask his mother, "Why aren't Rosie and the baby here?" He hoped they were both at the farm house, anxiously awaiting him.

Jake stepped up to his brother-in-law and greeted him, "Welcome home, soldier; we're sure happy to have you back with us. Janet and the boys are home, cooking up a big meal for you."

The fact that neither his mother nor Jake mentioned Rosie and the baby left Jimmie puzzled, confused, and in a state of apprehension. Where was Rosie? Why did she not come to meet him?

When Jake's car turned into the driveway of the large white Victorian house, Janet and her two boys came running out to meet Jimmie. The hugging, kissing, and crying started all over again.

As they approached the porch steps leading to the living room door, the door opened and Preacher Harris walked out. The preacher's presence made Jimmie anxious and uneasy. He asked, "Where is Dad?"

Janet threw her arms around her brother and cried, "Jimmie, Daddy is gone! He died of a massive heart attack."

"Why did you not mention it in your letters? Why would you keep it from me?" He was shedding tears for the third time this day.

Janet answered, "Jimmie, the day Daddy died you were on a ship going out to war. We just couldn't send you such upsetting news."

Jake took his two boys and went home for a while. The others entered the living room. Jimmie sat down in his father's favorite chair. He was very quiet. No one spoke.

Jane went into the kitchen to check on the turkey she had in the oven. It was the first week of March, but for the Cooper family it was a day of thanksgiving. Over nineteen thousand Marines died in the Pacific war. Some were shipped home to be buried in family plots; others were left behind in graves, marked and unmarked. But their Jimmie had come back to them, and they were grateful to the Almighty God.

After some time passed, Jimmie could hold back no longer: "Where is Rosie? Where is my son? And what's his name? Nobody wrote me his name!" Jimmie had hoped that Rosie would name their firstborn son James.

177

Preacher Harris moved his chair close to Jimmie's. What he had to tell the returning Marine this day was extremely difficult for him. He began, "Jimmie, the boy's name is Louis and he is not your son. The day you and Rosie were married, she already was pregnant with Louis Martel's child."

"Is she living with Louis now?" Jimmy asked.

"Not under the same roof, but gossipers and rumor mongers are saying there is an ongoing affair between them. They are also saying Rosie is planning to divorce you."

Jimmie just sat there, not saying anything. Preacher Harris went on, "Jimmie, you must forget Rosie. There are many nice girls in our church and young widows whose husbands died overseas. Any one of them would make you a good wife."

Jimmie didn't respond. He just sat there, staring into space. The preached asked, "Jimmie, are you all right?" Jimmie nodded yes.

Preacher Harris rose to leave. Nellie walked him to the door. "Nellie, bring Jimmie to the prayer service tomorrow night," he told her as he walked out the door.

Janet called her husband, and Jake and the boys returned for dinner. It was delicious. The turkey was nicely browned, juicy and tender. There were candied sweet potatoes with apples, mashed potatoes with giblet gravy, a large relish plate, cranberries, buttermilk biscuits, and pumpkin pie with whipped cream. Only Jake and the boys ate with hearty appetites. Jimmie ate very little, said he wasn't hungry.

Janet and her family left; Nellie and Jimmie settled down in the living room for the evening; he in his father's overstuffed brown leather chair and his mother in the matching rocker. Jake had built a fire in the wood-burning stove. The bright yellow flames were flickering; the room was cozy.

178

Jimmie looked around the room at the portraits of his parents and grandparents in their large ornate gilded frames hanging on the floral papered walls. He wondered if he would ever be a grandfather, even a father. He looked at the large oak table desk where he did his homework and remembered the day when he had spread out all his valentines to select the prettiest one for Rosie.

Jimmie came out of his daydreaming and asked his mother, "Mother, did you sell Dad's car?"

"Yes, we sold it shortly after your last furlough, but Jake found us a low-mileage 1938 DeSoto. Your father really loved driving that car. We saved it for you. Jake took it last week for a checkup, and it's in good running condition."

Since both mother and son were very tired at the end of this eventful day, they retired to bed early. The warm comfort of sleeping in his own bed again was soothing, and soon Jimmie was sound asleep.

He got up early the next morning. His mother was still asleep when he walked out to the barnyard. The cattle were all gone. They were sold at auction after his father died. He walked into the hay barn where he and Rosie used to slide down the hay rope, and he walked along the banks of the Black River. The boards from the raft he and Rosie had paddled on the river were laying on top of a pile of tree stumps. Small patches of snow still covered the hills where he and Rosie raced their sleds.

The aroma of frying bacon brought Jimmie back to the house. He poured himself a cup of freshly brewed coffee. He had forgotten how good a cup of coffee could taste.

After breakfast, he said to his mother, "I'm going to take the car out for a spin."

"Want me to go with you?" she asked.

"No, I just want to look around a bit. I won't be gone long."

179

Jimmie's first stop was the Mount Joy Cemetery, where his father was buried. "Beloved husband and father," the inscription read. He noted that his father would have been fifty-eight years old in April. Jimmie's mother's name and birth date were already on the tombstone.

On his way home, he stopped at his grandparents' homestead. The long-abandoned old house was still standing. The bleeding hearts his grandmother had planted were still there, their tender shoots popping out of the cold ground.

Janet and her family lived across the road from the old Cooper homestead. Jimmie stopped in for a visit with his sister. Her boys were in school, her husband out in the woods, cutting down cedars for fence posts. He was glad to find his sister at home alone. There was so much he wanted to talk to her about; so many questions he wanted to ask.

Janet made a pot of coffee and brought out a plate of gingersnaps, Jimmie's favorite cookie. They sat down at the small dinette table in her sunny country kitchen.

Jimmie and Janet discussed their mother's coping with living alone, her health, and her financial situation. They shared stories of friends from high school days, and Janet brought her brother up-to-date on them all. They browsed through Janet's scrapbooks of newspaper clippings of Mason County boys who served in the armed forces and those who did not return from the wars. And they talked about Rosie and the impending divorce.

The deep love that Jimmie carried in his heart for Rosie, Rosie felt for Louis Martel. Louis had hurt her on many a date, both physically and emotionally. He had used her for sexual gratification; then denied the son he had fathered. He made her the laughingstock of the community and drove her into marriage with a man she did not love; yet she could not stop loving Louis. She would not give up her trysts with

the flamboyant, passionate lover for a life with the quiet, tender-loving Jimmie.

Rosie was now a waitress at Charlie's Place. She began working there when her baby was four months old, and her mother agreed to take care of her grandson. During the war years, Rosie was popular with the servicemen who came to the bar, not only to drink but also to dance with the beautiful, vivacious girl. She helped to make Charlie's place one of the most profitable bars in Mason County.

Charlie's wife died shortly before the war ended. He lost interest in working long hours in the business. During the morning hours, Rosie was left in charge. She opened up the place at ten o'clock; but on some days she came in earlier. On those early mornings Louis, in his burgundy roadster with the yellow wheels, was parked back of the bar, waiting for her.

Louis Martel never married. He was engaged for a while to Jane Roberts, whose father owned a garment factory in Mason. The engagement broke up when Jane discovered that Louis was cheating on her with a barmaid.

While the men of Mason County between the ages of twenty-one and thirty-six, were being called into service, Louis stayed home. His father had gotten him an agricultural deferment. Louis, senior, told the draft board that he needed his son to help him run his large cattle ranch. He also paid each board member "a little on the side" to make sure the deferment was granted.

Hardly a day passed when someone did not call Nellie Cooper to pass on to her some rumor or a bit of gossip that she had picked up about Rosie. Nellie kept it all to herself.

Jimmie had been home for two weeks before he decided to visit Charlie's Place. He got there shortly after nine-thirty, but the place was still closed. He drove down the street, back of the bar, and saw the burgundy car with the yellow wheels.

He was amazed at the condition of the old Plymouth road-ster. It looked like new. But then he remembered that the Martels owned a car dealership, which included Plymouths, and had a large garage to service the cars they sold.

Jimmie sat in his car, reading the newspaper. Promptly at ten o'clock, the sign with the neon lights went on, indicating that Charlie's Place was open for customers.

Both Rosie and Louis were startled when Jimmie walked into the bar.

"What are you doing here?" Louis asked Jimmie.

"I came to see Rosie," Jimmie answered.

"I don't think she wants to see you," Louis replied.

"You keep out of this. This is just between me and my wife!" Jimmie shouted.

"Your wife? That's a laugh. She only married you for the allotment. Didn't want you back, either, so she could get ten thousand dollars."

Rosie kept her distance. She was ready to run out the back door if it was necessary.

Stunned at what he had just heard, Jimmie walked out of the bar and went home.

Nellie said that the Jimmie who walked out the door that morning was not the same person who returned home. He appeared extremely upset and went directly upstairs to his room. When she went up to see what the problem was, Jimmie yelled at her, "Mother, just leave me alone!"

Nellie had invited Janet and her family to a roast beef dinner that evening. When they arrived, Jimmie was still up in his room. The two nephews, both in their preteens, ran up to see their uncle. When they came down to join the family, all three had their arms full. Jimmie had given the boys a pile of comic books that he had collected when he was their age, his box of Cracker Jack prizes, a checkers set, even his baseball cap, mitt, and balls.

The boys ran up to their parents, shouting with joy, "Look what Uncle Jimmie gave us! He says we can have anything in his room we want."

Jimmie ate very little, didn't want to talk, excused himself before the meal was over, and went back upstairs to his room.

For two days his mother tried to figure out what was eating away at her son. She told her daughter, "He's like a ticking time bomb, ready to explode. I called Preacher Harris, but when he came Jimmie refused to see him."

After moping in his room for two days, Jimmie left the house early one morning without saying anything to his mother as to where he was going or when he would be returning. He took with him the Colt pistol he had brought back with him from the Pacific. The pistol, a powerful man-stopper, required a good deal of training to use it to full effect—Jimmie had that training. He got into the DeSoto and headed for Charlie's Place.

Jimmie parked his car alongside the Plymouth roadster and entered the bar through the back door. Rosie was sitting at a table near the door, having a cup of coffee. She heard the door open and saw him coming in. She could see that he was hiding something behind his right hip. Rosie stood up, ready to run for the front door. At that precise moment, with the master marksmanship of a Marine rifleman, Jimmie shot Rosie straight through the heart. He then turned around and went back out to the parking lot.

Jimmie opened the passenger side door of the Plymouth roadster. He sat down, with his legs dangling over the side of the seat, placed the revolver to his head, and fired, spewing his brains over the meticulously kept interior of Louis Martel's pride and joy.

Louis was in the stockroom, getting some supplies out for Rosie, when he heard the gunshot. He ran out and saw

Rosie on the floor, bleeding. He called for the ambulance and the sheriff. When they arrived, Rosie was already dead.

The sheriff and his deputy went to the Cooper home to see Nellie. They had already contacted Janet, and she was there with her mother. The officers asked to see Jimmie's room. On a small table, by his bedside, they found a letter:

My dear loved ones,

Do not grieve for me. I go to a better place. I am taking Rosie with me. Bury us in the two lots across the road from Daddy's grave site.

Mother, remember all those bleeding hearts Grandmother had growing around her house? They are still there. Dig up two plants, one for each side of our tombstone.

I will be watching over you all from up above.

All my love,

Jimmie

Along with the note was a receipt for a red granite tombstone; the inscriptions to be used were printed on a separate piece of paper with only the dates of death missing. The insurance policy was the original one Jimmie had received when he first entered the Marines. It listed his mother as the beneficiary. Whether he forgot to make a change after his marriage or if he deliberately chose not to no one will ever know.

Both caskets were closed. The visitation was only for the families. As the small group of people stood around the two caskets in the cemetery, listening to the words of Preacher Harris, a couple stood in the background, apart from the group. They were Louis Martel, Sr., and his wife, Josephine. Both were watching a little boy, who would soon be four years old, standing with his maternal grandmother, tightly

holding onto her hand. They both agreed that the boy was their grandson, Louis Martel III. They waited to talk to Mary Jensen after the grave site ceremony was over.

That night little Louis slept in a beautiful big mansion, in a bedroom in which his father had slept when he was a little boy. At first, the child was apprehensive; but there were so many toys for him to play with, people who had time to read stories to him, who doted on him, and a little Yorkshire puppy all his own. He was sheltered from any contacts with Rosie's family, even the grandmother. Rumor was that she had been paid well to give up all rights to him.

The Martels had not seen their son since the morning of the tragic shootings. He never returned home that day. Weeks later, they received a letter from him. He was in California. He had enlisted in the navy.

For the young woman with a child, the allotment had been a godsend; for the emotionally wounded Marine, it was a curse; for their families, it became a tragedy of the greatest magnitude.

Bibliography for Historical Facts

Leckie, Robert. *Challenge for the Pacific—the Struggle for Guadalcanal.* New York: Doubleday, 1965.

Fighting Elite: US Marine Corps 1941–45 Reed International Books, London: Rottman, Gordon, and Mike Chappell, 1955.

Sammy

The little white puppy ran around and round the blue-striped shirt hanging on the clothesline. He yelped and jumped and tried in vain to reach one of the sleeves as the shirt fluttered back and forth in the breeze. Just then, a gust of wind blew the clothes pole down. The clothes flew up in the air, somersaulted, then flopped low, touching the ground. The puppy jumped and grabbed a cuff between his level white teeth. At that moment, standing there on his hind feet, with cute little prick ears, black nose and lips, and a pure white coat, he looked more like a baby polar bear than a member of the canine family. Another gust of wind and the clothes flew away again, but this time the puppy held a cuff of the blue-striped shirt in his strong jaws. He dropped the cuff, sounded off with some shrill yelps, picked it up again, and ran toward the back porch, where he lay down to rest with his prize.

His name was Sammy and he was ten weeks old. He was the only puppy left of a litter of five born to Queenie, a purebred Samoyed. The other four had left for new homes before they were eight weeks old. Sammy, like the others, had been asked for long before he was born.

"If Queenie has any all-white males in the next litter, save one for me," John Richards asked his neighbor George Barnes, but over two months went by and Richards still had not come for the puppy.

Sammy dropped the cuff on the porch and stretched his paws over it. His tongue hung out and he was panting hard when the screen door creaked. He turned his head toward the door. Sarah Barnes, carrying a brown wicker basket in one hand and a red-checked clothespin bag in the other, came out on the porch. Sammy ran toward her and jumped up on her skirt. He tried to lick her hands, but she pushed him away.

"Down! Sammy, down! You're gonna tear my skirt!" Sarah shouted at the puppy.

Sammy returned for the cuff, then dropped it at Sarah's feet and looked up for her approval, his plumed tail wagging rhythmically, but she screamed at him, "You bad dog!" and headed for the flyswatter hanging near the screen door. Before she could pick it up, Sammy jumped off the porch and was back at the clothesline, running round and round the blue-striped shirt.

Sarah called out to her husband, "George! George! Come out and see what the puppy's done now."

"Don't get so excited," George answered from the rocking chair in the kitchen where he was smoking his pipe and looking over the *Monthly Farm Review*. "He's just a young pup and wants to play."

"Play? Just come and see what he's playing with! The cuff off your best shirt, that's what he's playing with."

George came out on the porch. He took the pipe out of his mouth, tapped it a couple of times against the palm of his hand, and looked at the cuff.

"Reckon, I'll have to call Richards and see why he ain't picking up his dog. Said he wanted an all-white male. . . . saved him the best one in the litter."

"Don't bother calling; just take him over there. If he don't want him, why don't he say so? Plenty round here that'll take him."

"Probably wants to get rid of the old dog first."

187

"Well, that's his problem. We can't keep this pup around any longer. Today it's the shirt; yesterday, the curtains; last week, the rubber plant. I tell you, you just gotta get rid of him before he tears this house to pieces. Honestly, sometimes I wish Queenie was a mongrel; then we could just drown the litters and not have to save dogs for everyone in the county!"

"I don't want to make a special trip with him," George answered.

"You gotta go to town today with the cream and eggs. Take him, then. I tell you, George, you just gotta get that dog out of here before I go crazy."

"Guess I can take him then. Good a time as any with Queenie and the boys down at the creek. Sure some beautiful rainbows under that bridge. Maybe I'll take time to go down there myself."

"Never mind the rainbows; get rid of the dog!" Sarah picked up the basket and headed for the clothesline. "Honestly, look at that! He's even pulled down the line," she muttered to herself as she picked up the pole and propped up the line again.

George loaded two crates of eggs and a five-gallon can of cream into his black Ford truck, then looked around for a cardboard box large enough to hold the puppy. He found one just the right size and with his pocketknife cut two round holes, about the size of a saucer, on each end. He whistled and the puppy came running.

"This is it, Sammy boy; you're gonna have a new home tonight," George told the puppy as he patted him on the head and placed him in the box. Sammy had never been in such close quarters before. He began to whimper.

When George arrived at the Richards Farm, he remained in the truck and looked around for John Richards, a tall, slightly stooped, graying man of seventy years, who always wore blue suspender overalls two sizes too large and an old straw hat. When George didn't see him anywhere, he blew the horn but made no attempt to leave the truck. The black-and-white sign in the driveway, BEWARE OF DOG, was a warning to all who entered the premises not to move unless one of the Richards came out to greet them.

In the forty years the Richards had lived on the farm, they had always had a "biting dog." Canis Major, their current dog—a silvery-haired German shepherd—had the reputation of being the most vicious dog in the township. The Richards didn't like to talk about the incidents, but Ida Sargent, the local hypochondriac, always knew who was the latest victim and exactly how it happened. When not sitting in Dr. Farrell's office, Ida spent her time reporting all the newsy items she had heard on her last visit on the party line phone. Everyone knew all about Canis Major.

John Richards was greasing his tractor behind the toolshed and when he heard the horn blow; Canis Major was out in the cow pasture when he heard the car turning into the driveway. He and his master arrived at the same time, Canis barking ferociously, Richards trying to calm him down.

"It's all right Canis; now you just quiet down. It's all right, Canis," Richards repeated over and over again.

Finally Canis walked away and lay down under the lilac bush near the driveway. He still continued to bark, but the barking was sporadic and less ferocious.

Barnes rolled down the window and called out, "Got the dog with me! . . . Still want him?"

"Glad you brought 'em, George. I would've picked him up a couple weeks ago of it weren't for all that gas disappearing around here," Richards answered. "Someone sure is siphoning it off. That's all anyone talked about at the stock yards last week."

189

"Did you lose any?" George asked.

"Nope, not a drop. It's Canis Major that's keeping them away. Best watchdog we ever had. He won't let anyone out of a car unless Jennie or I are right there."

"You're sure lucky to have a dog like Canis. My gas tank went down mighty fast this last time. Our Queenie makes up with everyone. She even wagged her tail at the bum who strayed from the tracks last summer. Frightened Sarah half to death. But that's a Samoyed for you. They're noted for being good-natured and affectionate."

Richards looked down at the ground and kicked a small stone from under his foot. "Sure hate to do away with that dog. We've had him for five years and both Jennie and I have become terribly attached to him."

"Why would you want to do away with him?" George asked.

"He's taken to chasing sheep. Sheriff says either Canis goes or we pay for all the dead sheep around here."

"Well, once they get to chasing sheep you'd better get rid of 'em quick. They sure can bring you a heap of trouble."

"It's that damn bitch on the Russell place! She's the one that got him started. I tell you, for three years Canis never strayed any more than to chase a car up the road now and then. But the day he met up with that mongrel, we've had trouble ever since."

"You haven't tried to confine him so that he can't get away?"

"We have tried, but nothing has worked out. We locked him in the woodshed. He dug a hole under the door and took off. We put him in a fenced-in area. He dug himself out. He can pull out a stake, chew up a harness, and pull his head out of a collar."

George tried to sympathize with "Well, that's the way it goes sometimes. By the way, how'd you ever come up with a name like Canis Major?"

Richards laughed. "Everybody asks that. You know, that Jennie of mine is quite a stargazer, always looking up at the sky. She's the one thought up the name."

"Oh, I remember now. The dogs of Orion—Canis Major, the great dog, and Canis Minor, the little dog. They're somewhere around the Milky Way, aren't they?"

"They're southern constellations separated by the Milky Way. Did you know that one of the brightest stars in the heavens is situated in Canis Major? It's the dog star, Sirius. At first, Jennie couldn't quite make up her mind whether to name him Sirius or Canis Major, but she finally decided on Canis Major . . . said she knew then and there that he would be a great dog."

"I hear he's considered the best watchdog around here" George answered.

"He's not only a good watchdog, but he's a good working dog. He'll go into the woods and bring the cows home for milking all by himself. Last week one of 'em broke through the fence into the potato patch and he went right in after her. He knows when they're in place they're not supposed to be! We haven't lost any chickens since we've had him, either. Barks a mad streak at a cruising hawk and kills any coon that has the audacity to poke his nose around here. Even separates the cats when they're fighting."

Richards kicked another stone from under his feet and began fidgeting with his suspenders.

George looked down at his watch. "Guess I better get going or I'm going to be late getting home for chores."

Richards looked up at the westward-moving sun and answered, "Yep, it's getting around that time, ain't it? Time sure goes. Can't get much done these days."

George turned toward the back of the truck where Sammy was quivering in the box. "You wanna take him out of the box?" he asked.

"No, I'll let him be till Jennie gets home. She's gone to one of them Ladies' Aid Meetings." Richards lifted the box with the dog out of the truck."Sure a pretty dog, ain't he? What'd you say his name was?"

"We called him Sammy because he's the only one in the litter that looks like a Samoyed."

"He's not purebred, then?" Richards asked.

"No, his mother is, but I couldn't tell you about the father. Could be most any dog around here, even Canis."

Richards shook his head. "Just can't ever be another Canis. Ain't ever had a dog like him before, never expect to again!"

"I wouldn't say that," George answered. "I know you'll learn to love Sammy. The Samoyed's an intelligent, hard-working dog. With proper training, he'll turn out a dog that you'll be proud to own."

Richards set the box with Sammy on the porch. Canis immediately came to sniff at the little puppy, who was whimpering and trying to get out of the box. Richards took Canis by the collar and walked him to his kennel. He picked up the chain and slipped it on the collar, then unhooked the chain from its anchored place and walked Canis to the plowed field back of the kennel. Canis dropped his tail low and began to drag his feet. Richards gave him a little shove and guided him to a fence post, where he fastened the cable. Walking briskly, he returned to the house and a few minutes later came out carrying his deer rifle.

Canis was no stranger to guns. He had been shot at several times, the most recently by a game warden while chasing deer with a neighbor's dog on state land. Both dogs got away, but their owners received stern warnings to keep the dogs confined. Canis spotted the gun and recognized trouble. He tried to pull away from his leash, but the time was too short. Richards loaded the gun, took careful aim, and fired. Sammy watched through the opening in his box. He heard Canis Major let out a long, mournful whine and saw him roll on his side. His dark brown eyes remained open and fixed on his master to the end. Sammy began to whimper uncontrollably.

Richards heard the car come up the driveway and hurried with the last few shovels of dirt. He met Jennie as she came out of the garage.

"Got a surprise for you," he said.

"Tom and Susie?" she asked, looking around for the grandchildren.

"No. Guess again," he told her.

But before Jennie could guess again, Sammy let out with some shrill yelps and the surprise was over. Jennie walked over to the box and looked in.

"Oh, John, he's adorable!" she cried out and lifted the puppy out of the box. She placed him over her shoulder as if she were going to burp him. When she patted Sammy on the head, he wagged his tail and licked her hair, which was only a shade darker than his own white coat.

"Well, Jennie, you think he's all right?"

"He's just like a little teddy bear! You don't suppose he's part polar bear, do you?" she asked.

Richards laughed, "Hardly think so. He's a Samoyed. Some of his ancestors might have been around the polar regions. Explorers have used the Samoyed in expeditions to both the Arctic and Antarctic regions."

Suddenly Mrs. Richards remembered that Canis did not run out to meet her when she pulled into the yard. "John, where's Canis?" she asked.

Richards hesitated for a moment. "He's gone, Jennie. Got it over with just before you came. It's best this way. He was bound to bring us trouble."

Mrs. Richards did not say a word. She continued gently stroking Sammy as she carried him into the house. They blocked off a section of the kitchen with cardboard boxes and covered the floor with newspapers. A faded old blanket rolled into an oblong pad provided a bed for the puppy. The excitement of the new home was exhausting for Sammy; the heat from the wood-burning stove made his corner warm and cozy. He explored his new quarters, sniffing at everything. Then he stretched out on the blanket and fell asleep.

Richards went out to the barn to milk his herd of Holsteins while his wife busied herself with the preparation of their evening meal. Soon the tantalizing aroma of frying chicken permeated the kitchen and awakened Sammy. He yawned, he stretched, and he yawned again. Then he headed for the small white bowl of milk that had been set out for him. He lapped up all the milk and whined for more. When he was ignored, he returned to his pad for another nap.

When Sammy awakened from the second nap, the kitchen was very dark and very quiet. He heard faint rocking sounds in the distance and saw a ray of light coming from the living room, where the Richardses had settled for the evening. John was sitting at his desk, totalling the monthly milk receipts; Jennie, leaning back in the Early American platform rocker, was joining together crocheted squares of shiny black yarn with bright red rose centers. The nearly completed afghan lay draped over her knees and hung all around the rocker. At frequent intervals she stopped working and gently rocked back and forth, gazing at her masterpiece. It was during one of those intervals that Sammy woke up and discovered he was all alone in the kitchen. He began to cry. At first quietly, then louder.

"Aha! There he goes," Richards said to his wife. "I knowed it all along. It's just like having a baby in the house."

"Think we should let him out for a spell?" she asked.

194

"No, leave him be. He'll feel more secure in his own little corner than running all around the house," he answered.

Sammy's crying persisted. Finally Mrs. Richards could stand it no longer. "I'll just take a look at him," she said. The moment she turned on the kitchen light, Sammy began to wag his tail.

Mrs. Richards smiled. "Just want a little attention, don't you? Probably hungry, too."

Sammy answered with a yelp, a jump, and a whine, his tail wagging all the while. His bowl got refilled with scraps of chopped chicken, and he also got a bowl of fresh water. While he was eating, Mrs. Richards filled a hot water bottle and placed it on his pad. Sammy's hunger was now satisfied, and the soft rubber bottle of water made him feel that he had someone with him. He quieted down for the rest of the night.

During his first week with the Richardses, Sammy ate four meals a day at four-hour intervals. He slept in the quarters behind the stove at night. During the day he followed Jennie around, tagging at her heels. He played with the long streamers of her half-apron and pulled at the white petticoat, which often hung an inch or more below her dress all the way around. But he enjoyed most of all the times they both left the house and went out in the yard. There was so much to explore. There were perils, too, as the day he first met Brownie and her brood. When Sammy just stood there, looking them over, the old hen didn't mind, but the moment he nuzzled one of her fuzzy yellow chicks she sprang at him, giving him a severe lashing with her wings and inflicting several pecks on his head and nose before Mrs. Richards could shoo her away.

Sammy became acquainted with Woolie, a gray-and-white tabby tomcat almost the size of Sammy. Woolie was a prowler and hunter. Once the sun went down, he left the premises; but during the day, he liked to curl up on an old braided rug on the back porch and sleep the day away. When Woolie was not sleeping, he was preening himself, and the white patches on his coat were as white as the milk he drank. Woolie was accustomed to dogs. He had gotten along with Canis and knew all the neighboring dogs, since in his prowls he often strayed far away from home and was gone for a week or more. He paid no attention to Sammy.

Woolie returned from one of his night jaunts one morning very thirsty. He headed for the back porch, where Mr. Richards had just filled a white bowl with fresh milk. When Sammy spotted the cat drinking from the bowl, he went wild. He barked and he growled and he snapped at Woolie, but Woolie wouldn't even raise his head until he'd had his fill of milk. The commotion brought Mr. Richards out on the porch.

"Why, Sammy, that's not your bowl! You leave Woolie alone." He picked up the puppy and took him in the house. As soon as he let him down, Sammy ran to the back door and whined to be let out. The Richardses were ready to sit down to breakfast and let him out so they could eat in peace.

Woolie was still on the porch, grooming his long bushy tail. The tail fascinated Sammy. He tried to play with it as he did with Mrs. Richards' apron strings. Woolie retaliated by hissing and spitting at Sammy, but that didn't stop the puppy. The tomcat then slapped Sammy, first with one paw, then the other, each time with all the claws exposed. The scratches hurt Sammy. He whimpered and jumped back. Woolie's tail was now wagging back and forth in a semicircle. This fascinated Sammy all the more, and he grabbed the tail again. Woolie ran off the porch and headed for the woodpile nearby. The puppy was right behind him. Woolie scampered up the pile of cedar slabs and, when he reached the top, stretched himself out and began to sharpen his claws on one of the slabs of wood. Sammy ran around the woodpile several times, trying to find a place where he might scale the woodpile, but all he succeeded in doing was loosening one of the slabs, which fell on his head, leaving a two-inch cut.

Mrs. Richards came out of the house hurriedly, grabbed Sammy, not too gently, under his front legs, and took him back in the house. She dropped him in the corner. "You bad dog! You're gonna stay here till we finish breakfast." It was the same tone of voice Mrs Barnes had used with Sammy when he tore the cuff off the shirt and many other times. He gave Mrs. Richards one of his mournful looks and retreated to his cushion.

Mrs. Richards returned to the breakfast table. "John, Sammy has a rather bad cut on his head," she said.

"Woolie probably scratched him," he replied.

"He has scratches, too, but this is quite a bad cut."

"I'll take a look at him when I'm finished eating. Looks like he's gonna be more trouble than he's worth," Richards said gloomily, and he poured himself another cup of coffee.

"Want me to hunt up something for a bandage?" Mrs. Richards asked.

"No, he wouldn't like it. But you can get out that small collar we had for Canis when he was a pup."

"You're not going to keep him tied up?"

"Well, I'm not gonna have him run loose and have that bitch leading this one astray."

"Oh, didn't I tell you? Old man Mason shot her."

"Where did you hear that?"

"On the party line. I though I told you about it."

"First I've heard of it! How did that come about?"

"I don't know. When I picked up the receiver, I heard Mason say, 'Okay, Sheriff, if you're coming out right away, I'll leave her right where she fell.' Then the sheriff asked,

'You sure it's the Russell dog?' and Mason answered, 'As sure as my name is Mason!' "

"Well, I'll be darned. That's the best thing that old codger ever did. Too bad he didn't do it sooner," Richards replied.

"John, you really think he was trying to pin the whole thing on Canis?"

"Darn tootin', that's what he was working at. Someone must've told him we got rid of Canis."

"News always travels fast around here," Mrs. Richards answered.

She went up in the attic and came down with some old towels; meanwhile, Richards spread an oilcloth over the kitchen table and filled a gray enamel basin with warm water. He went to pick up Sammy from his pad, but the puppy backed away from him and growled. From the first day of his arrival at the Richards home, Sammy accepted Jennie, but he refused to have anything to do with John. John was puzzled by the rejection; then he remembered seeing the puppy looking out from the cut-out slot of the cardboard box the day Canis was killed. Sammy had seen John pull the reluctant Canis to the stake, where he had chained him, then shot him. The puppy had heard the long, mournful whine of the dying dog as he rolled on his side. John decided to leave the task of tending to Sammy's wounds to Jennie and assist only as needed.

As soon as Sammy's wounds healed, he was given a brown leather collar, taken out to the kennel, and chained for the first time. The chain, fastened to a heavy overhead wire between two apple trees, gave the puppy plenty of space to run around. When he became accustomed to the new quarters, he no longer was confined to the kennel area during the day; however, every night, just before the Richards retired, he was "tied up for the night."

Every morning at six-thirty, Sammy was released and followed the Richardses to the barn. There he sat on the threshold until the milking was completed and they all returned to the house for breakfast. After breakfast, he roamed around the yard. Once in a while, he ran off as far as the pasture but never strayed away from the home grounds long enough to be missed.

Sammy adored Mrs. Richards. The moment she walked out of the house, he was right at her heels. She taught him the meaning of "sic 'em." Any hawk cruising over the chicken yard was pointed out to Sammy with "sic 'em," and the puppy learned to respond by looking toward the sky and barking until the hawk flew away. A chicken scratching around the flower beds was sure to have Sammy sicced at her, and not one ever got away. He chased the chicken until he cornered her against the fence, then held her there until Mrs. Richards picked her up and heaved her back over the fence where she belonged. Even old Molly, the leader of the Holstein herd, knew that "sic 'em" meant Sammy snapping at her heels. Molly had a reputation for breaking down fences into cornfields. It became Sammy's duty to get her back into the pasture.

Sammy accompanied Mrs. Richards whenever she went into the woods looking for mushrooms or wild berries. These were exciting times for him. There was always some squirrel to send up a tree or a gopher to chase back into his burrow. Sometimes they came upon a flock of wild turkeys, which Sammy promptly scattered in all directions, forcing them to seek shelter in the branches of the tallest trees. Sammy had now become acquainted with most of the animals inhabiting the Richards' 160-acre farm. He had not, however, seen another dog since the day he left his mother and the home of George and Sarah Barnes.

One late September afternoon, Mrs. Richards was looking around among the fallen leaves for fall mushrooms and Sammy, not finding anything to chase, was lying down near the basket. Suddenly he stood up, very alert. He sounded off with a short bark. At first, Mrs. Richards ignored him, but when he continued with short sporadic barks and didn't move from his place, she became interested.

"What is it, Sammy?" she asked.

Sammy barked again and wagged his tail.

"Oh, it's someone you know," she said. "John, is that you?" she called out. There was a rustling of leaves behind one of the small evergreens.

"Must be Woolie," Mrs. Richards said to Sammy. "Woolie? Woolie?" she kept calling. But it was not Woolie who came out from behind the bushes. . . . It was a small cocker spaniel with long ears and shiny black curly fur. The black dog did not bark but just stood there, watching Sammy. Sammy wagged his tail, but he didn't move, either.

"Oh, no! It can't be," Mrs. Richards cried out. She picked up a piece of loose stump and threw it at the black dog. "G'wan home! Sic 'em; sic 'em, Sammy!" she shouted.

But Sammy wouldn't sic 'em. He barked and pranced around in his original spot, but he would not chase the black curly-haired dog.

Mrs. Richards picked up the mushroom basket and grabbed Sammy by the collar. "Come on, Sammy. We gotta see Mr. Richards."

John Richards was out on the north forty sowing winter wheat. He noticed Mrs. Richards and Sammy, in the distance, coming toward him. He stopped the tractor, jumped off, and walked toward them.

"Whatta you two doing way out here?" he asked.

"John, you'll never guess what I just saw," Mrs. Richards answered, breathless from the long fast walk.

"Bear?" he asked.

"Worse than that—a black dog. It's a spitting image of the other one, but smaller. If it were the same size, I'd swear Mason never shot her."

"Where did you see it?"

"Back of the big hill, where all those stumps are," she answered.

"That's close enough to be one of the Russells' dogs. Might've known with a female around there was bound to be a litter. It must be one of her offspring."

"Sure looks like it. I don't know of anybody else around here having a black cocker spaniel."

"Those spaniels are good sporting dogs. Could be they're training it for hunting. Sure there was no one around with her?"

"Not a soul. Sammy could've made a fuss if there had been. But you know what; he sure acted strangely, just like it was somebody he knew. He wagged his tail all the while."

"Probably another bitch," Richards answered in a disgusted tone of voice. "You know Canis used to be, ready to chew the head off any male who dared to show himself around, but that female could eat his dish out clean and he wouldn't even let a bark out of him."

Mrs. Richards went mushroom hunting one more time. She did not take Sammy with her. She didn't want to take the chance that he would meet up with the stray dog. It was still Indian summer, and the woods were beautiful, arrayed in different shades of reds and yellows, with a sprinkling of evergreens among them.

The Indian summer came to an abrupt end with the first snowfall and the onset of winter. The early winter lingered for a long time, and finally spring arrived. But the curly-haired black dog had not been seen again.

Sammy was a year old now and no longer a puppy. He stood twenty inches tall at the shoulder and weighed fifty pounds. His beautiful white fur had a thick and soft, short undercoat and a profuse hard-textured outer coat. He carried his long tail over his back when he was alert or full of action, but when he was at rest he often dropped it low. Sammy had grown into a beautiful dog, and the Richards were mighty proud of him.

Heavy spring rains washed away the last traces of snow. As soon as the rain-made rivers soaked into the ground, farmers went out into the fields. Tractors were rolling from early spring to late evening. Red gasoline trucks sped down the country roads, responding to calls for gasoline . . . and the gas thieves returned.

Farmer after farmer reported losses. A tractor that had broken down and was left in the field over the weekend had an empty gas tank Monday morning. Tractors that stood in lean-to sheds with no doors were found to be an easy target. The thieves were getting bolder. One of Richards' neighbors reported that his truck had been drained dry right in his own garage. The pattern was the same as it has been a year ago—a weekend job.

At that time, everyone suspected the Mason boys. Although Sheriff Bronson and his deputy kept a close check on the boys' activities for two months, they were not able to turn up any evidence that the Masons were the gasoline thieves. When Frankie Mason was reported as having been seen removing a box from a grocery delivery truck in town, the sheriff got a search warrant and he and his deputy combed every acre of the Mason farm, the house, barns, and other buildings. They did not find the stolen box. When they checked the Masons' gasoline storage tank, they found it was empty. The sheriff's vigil, however, did put an end to the gas siphoning for the rest of that summer and fall. Then the snows came and no thief could take the chance of being tracked. All was quiet.

Now the work season was in full swing. During the weekdays, the farmers worked late, stayed home evenings, and retired early; however, on Saturday nights it was the custom for families to come into town, bringing with them the eggs and cream and any other produce they had for sale. After selling their goods and stocking up on groceries and anything else they needed, the wives and children attended the weekly movie at the Cushing Circle Theater. The men all went to the North Side Inn to drink, shoot pool, or play cards. The North Side Inn had always been the liveliest place in town on Saturday nights. Suddenly it became deserted. The farmers were staying home Saturday nights, their lights out and their deer rifles loaded.

Gasoline thieves were keeping the farmers home on Saturday nights, but nothing could keep Cushing County families home Sunday mornings. They were churchgoing people, and the three churches in the county seat were filled to capacity every Sunday. The Richards drove ten miles for the ten o'clock services at St. Andrew's by the Lake. It was eleven-thirty when they returned home. As always on Sunday mornings, Sammy was locked in the shed adjoining the back of the house. The outside door of the shed was locked with a sliding bar from the inside, and the entrance from the house was through the kitchen. As soon as the Richards walked into the kitchen, they heard Sammy jumping up against the outside door and barking viciously. When John went to let him out, he found Sammy in a highly agitated state and foaming at the mouth. "What's happened here, Sammy?" he asked as he unlatched the door; but as soon as the latch was free Sammy slammed his body against the door and ran out. He headed for the woods.

"Sammy, you come back. Come back, you hear!"

Sammy just kept on running. Richards ran after him, but the dog soon disappeared from sight. He returned to the house and changed from his Sunday suit to his blue suspender overalls and a pair of knee-high rubber boots. Between the two hills of the wooded area lay a wide swamp of black muddy waters that came up well over the ankles. You needed rubber boots to cross it at any point. Since the area was all fenced in, the chances were that Sammy would still be found on home property.

Richards put on his straw hat and picked up his walking cane from its hook on the back porch. He always took the cane with him when he went walking in the woods. It made it easier for him to climb the steep hills. He followed along the cattle path through the pasture, whistling every few minutes for Sammy. When he had walked to the end of his property, he climbed over the fence and walked up the dusty dirt road a quarter of a mile till he came to the Mason property. He found a break in the fence and slid through it. It was easier than climbing over the fence. By the time he reached the hill overlooking the Masons' sheep pasture, he was puffing. He pulled a red handkerchief from one of the deep pockets of his overalls and wiped the perspiration beads running down his forehead. He stood there for a while, looking down into the valley. The sheep were grazing quietly. There wasn't a dog in sight.

On his way back, Richards walked all around his fence line, checking here and there for breaks in the fence and any loose posts. He had stopped to prop up a wobbly post when something caught his eye. *What in tarnation happened here?* he asked himself as he examined the fence around the loose post. The wires had been cut and the ends bent into hooks that slid easily into staples in the post, making it possible to open the fence like a gate. Upon examining the area more closely, Richards noticed tire tracks leading into his property. He followed the track and discovered that someone had backed a vehicle into the woods about thirty feet. He looked around for a pile of dumped trash but found none. Outside of the tracks, there was nothing unusual in the area.

Richards returned home without Sammy, still puzzled and mumbling to himself, "Sure can't understand it."

"Can't understand what?" Mrs Richards asked.

"Why anyone would cut the fence and back up some kind of a vehicle onto our property. Probably a pickup truck."

"Could have been poachers."

"I looked all around, didn't find any sign of a deer being dragged or bloodstains. Course with all those dead leaves and twigs around, they could have covered up."

"Is Sammy back?"

"Yes. He got back just a few minutes ago. Sure is panting. You know, come to think of it, when we came home from church, he was so hoarse he could hardly bark. You don't suppose we had visitors this morning?"

Richards bolted out the door and ran towards the gas tank. Sammy followed at his heels, barking. Richards opened the spout. A few drops of gas dribbled out—the tank was empty. "Son of a bitches! They're stealing gas while we're praying," Richards blurted out in anger. The question now was who? He returned to the house and called the sheriff.

"John, where is the fence cut? Is it back of the hill where all those stumps are?" Nellie asked.

"Why, yes, that's exactly where it is. How did you know?"

"That's where Sammy and I saw that black curly-haired dog last fall. The one we thought belonged to the Russells."

"I don't think the Russells would steal gas. They had some stolen from them last year. Maybe that bitch of theirs

205

had a litter in one of those hollow stumps and they went in to fetch her out. Whoever was there, was there this morning. Those were fresh tracks.''

The sheriff and his deputy arrived within the hour. The deputy checked the fence post for fingerprints and made a cast of the tire tracks. Richards and the sheriff walked around the large pine stumps. Some were rotted out, with only the outside shell remaining. Two had holes large enough for a bear's den. A third one had a piece of brown canvas stuck in it. The odor of gasoline permeated the area. The sheriff pulled out the canvas and exposed two five-gallon metal cans. Both were filled with gasoline.

"Don't leak a word of this to anyone," the sheriff warned Richards. "I'm sure it's the Mason boys, and we're gonna get 'em this time."

On the way back to their scout car, the two law men stopped at Sammy's kennel. "Sure a beautiful dog you got here," one of them remarked.

"Very smart, too," Richards answered. "If he hadn't run into the woods this morning, we never would have found that gas."

"I hope he doesn't take to chasing sheep like your other dog did," the sheriff answered.

"Canis had the run of the place. We're keeping Sammy confined; and if we're both going to be away, he gets locked up in the back shed."

"That's the wise thing to do. Once they get running, you can't break them of the habit."

"We never had any problem with Canis until that Russell bitch started coming around. It got to where as soon as she showed up, they ran off together. I think he would have followed her to hell if that's where she wanted to go."

The sheriff laughed. "You know, that Russell dog was shot on your property, not too far from where we found the gas today."

"You think Mason shot her because she discovered their hiding place for the stolen gas?"

"I am sure that's what happened."

The fingerprints found on the gasoline cans belonged to Frankie and Richard Mason. The tire tracks matched up with those of their pickup truck. The boys were arrested and lodged in the county jail. At the next meeting of the county draft board, both boys were included in the group of recruits leaving the county for the army induction center at Fort Custer.

The part Richards and Sammy played in the arrest of the Mason boys was never revealed. Both Richards and Sheriff Bronson felt that if the news ever leaked out, old man Mason would take revenge and shoot Sammy.

Sammy would never be taken into the woods again; but as time went by he was given more freedom. He no longer was leashed if one of the Richards was home but rarely strayed far from the home base. His favorite pastime was trying to dig critters out of their burrows, not only all around the old buildings but also in the nearby grain fields. But that was all to change and the change would come very soon. The son would stray the way of the father.

Sammy went to the barn with Richards for the morning milking as was his usual practices. Mrs. Richards followed when the cows were all in the barn. She missed Sammy immediately.

"John, did Sammy come with you to the barn this morning?" she asked.

"Yes, he was here just a few minutes ago. Isn't he here now?"

"I don't see him anywhere."

"He must have gone back to the house."

The Richards finished their milking and returned to the house. Sammy was not there. They both called him, but there was no response. He just seemed to have vanished. Richards picked up Sammy's leash and headed for the woods. He did not have to go far. Wild turkeys were squawking and flying up into the trees. The curly-haired black female dog was chasing the flock. Sammy had caught himself a young turkey hen and was lying down, holding the prize between his front paws. He wagged his tail as Richards approached him and fastened the leash to his collar; then resisted stubbornly, struggling against the leash, jolting and jerking all the way home.

"There goes your freedom," Richards told him as he removed the leash and fastened him to the chain on his doghouse. He then went in the house and called Jake Russell.

"Jake, we have a problem! I found our dogs together this morning, chasing turkeys on the back forty that joins the Masons' sheep pasture. I just brought Sammy home and chained him. Did your cocker spaniel come home?"

"I didn't know she was missing. We have her fenced in a dog run. She must have dug herself out. I'll have to go find her. Thanks."

The Richards' sat down to a breakfast of pancakes and sausage. Both were very upset. Just when they thought they had a dog who would not stray far from home, this happened.

"I think George Barnes was right when he said that Canis may be Sammy's father. He looks a great deal like Queenie, but he doesn't have the smiling face and gentleness of the Samoyed mother. Every day I see more of Canis in his personality. He's got his intelligence and alertness; but most of all, I see in him the self-confidence and aloofness that were so evident in Canis."

Jennie agreed and added, "I sure hate to see him leashed all the time. He was such a happy dog, running and exploring all around the old buildings."

"I have been thinking for some time about new fencing for the area around the house, gardens, and orchard. That would give him a large area for running during the day and we would only have to leash him for the night."

"When are you going to find the time to take on that kind of a project?"

"I'll just have to sneak in a day here and there between the haying, harvesting, and threshing."

"Maybe one of your brothers could give you a hand on weekends."

"They probably both could. The steel mill is closed on Saturday and Sunday."

John's two older brothers lived thirty miles from the farm and worked in a steel mill in town. They never turned down an invitation to return to the farm where they had been born and worked the land with their father. John was the youngest and remained on the farm after the father died. Jennie always cooked up a feast for them of her crispy fried chicken, stuffed pork chops, or a fancy roast. She made delicious apple pies and devil's food cakes, too. They always said it was worth a trip to the farm just to stay for the dinner.

With three men working on the project, by the time the leaves came down at the end of October the area was all fenced in and the gates were all up. And Sammy ran around the area exploring every nook and cranny. But if the Richards were both going to be away for a long time, he was still locked in the back shed. It was all working very well.

November second brought the first accumulation of snow for the season. It started snowing during the night, and by morning five inches lay on the ground. When Sammy didn't come out to the barn with them, the Richards' assumed that he didn't like the snow and was sleeping in his well-insulated kennel. Returning back to the house, they noticed tracks around the gate leading to the back forty and the woods. Sammy was nowhere to be seen, and John went to investigate. He discovered dogs had been digging under the steel gate from each side. Sammy got out and both sets of tracks headed for the woods. Richards followed the tracks that zigzagged around the field, then headed toward the Masons' sheep pasture. Looking down into the pasture from the hill on his property, he saw the large herd of Shropshire rams, ewes, and lambs bleating in utter confusion with Sammy and the black cocker spaniel chasing them all around the sheds and pasture. Some of the animals were trying to get into the sheds and were piling up at the doors.

In rapid succession, two shots rang out from behind one of the sheds and the two dogs started running back to the woods. Another shot rang out. The cocker spaniel fell in the snow. Immediately, the white snow turned red around her. The gun went off again. This time, Sammy fell and Richards saw old man Mason walking back to his house. He ran down the hill and came upon the cocker spaniel first. She was bleeding profusely. She would not survive. Richards ran toward Sammy. Sammy was whimpering mournfully. He had been shot in one of the hind legs. He would have to be taken to the veterinarian. While Richards was pondering how to get the wounded dog, weighing fifty pounds, up the hill, Jake Russell, his son, and two grandsons arrived on the scene, pulling two toboggans.

The boys let go of their toboggans, and ran toward their pet, whom they both adored. "Princess! Oh, Princess!" they cried when they saw that she was already dead. Both dogs were transported to the Russell place on the toboggans, and Jake drove Richards home to get his pickup truck so he could take Sammy directly to the county animal clinic.

Mrs. Richards called on ahead before they left the house, and Dr. Clark was all set up for Sammy when they arrived. After the initial examination, there was a long consultation. Sammy's kneecap was completely shattered. He also had other injuries. The Richards had to make a decision—should the veterinarian try to save their dog or put him to sleep permanently? They chose treatment.

The healing process was slow. It was some time before Sammy returned home. He returned to his original pad behind the wood stove in the kitchen. When spring came, his kennel was moved to the back porch, but on warm sunny days he preferred the front porch and the mat in front of the entrance door.

Sammy had grown into a beautiful dog, and the Richards' loved him dearly. Visitors coming to the house for the first time were immediately attracted to the dog with the beautiful milk-white fur and plumed tail Their admiration quickly turned to pity when Sammy stood up to greet them. For never again would Sammy chase wild turkeys and squirrels into trees nor run around the fields and barns sending varmits into their burrows and then trying to dig them out. On that tragic cold and snowy November day when he lost his cocker spaniel playmate; Sammy also lost his left hind leg with the badly fractured kneecap.